BYKER

BYKER GROVE

·

ADELE ROSE

BBC BOOKS

Published by BBC Books
a division of BBC Enterprises Limited
Woodlands, 80 Wood Lane, London W12 0TT

First published 1989
© Adele Rose 1989
ISBN 0 563 20884 8

Reprinted 1990 (twice)

Set in 10/12pt Baskerville by Ace Filmsetting Ltd,
Frome Somerset
Printed in England by Clays Ltd, St Ives plc

CONTENTS

CHAPTER ONE

Julie Warner hated Newcastle. She didn't want to be in this ghastly part of the world at all. She might just as well have been on Mars. In fact she'd much *sooner* have been on Mars. And the giant Metro Shopping Centre, with all its trendy boutiques, bright lights and crowds of Saturday morning shoppers left her completely cold.

'Don't you think it's amazing, love?' Julie's father was doing his best to cheer her up. She scowled and kept her eyes firmly on the ground.

'There's all your favourite shops we had in London, Jule. Do you want to try that jacket on?' She shrugged as she followed him into the shop. Poor old Dad, he was wasting his time. The only thing that would cheer her up would be if they packed their bags and went back home where they belonged.

'Julie, sweet, it's really very nice here, if you'd only give it a chance. Go out, make some friends . . .'

'I've got friends. They're all at home.'

Mr Warner sighed. 'This is your home now. You're fourteen, you're not a child. You know the circumstances.'

'You could have said no.'

'I couldn't, love.' They reached the car. 'Tell you what, there's a place a chap at work told me about, Byker Grove. He said a lot of young people go there, they have a great time . . .'

But his words fell on stony ground. Julie threw her parcels on the back seat, and shut her ears to what her dad was saying. She didn't want to know about Byker Grove. She already knew it would be horrible. Just like the rest of this horrible place.

'Hiya!'

Donna Bell and Nicola Pearson sighed as a small red-haired girl hurtled through the crowd of shoppers like a tiny guided missile. Kirstie Campbell, known to one and all as Spuggie, was twelve (quite a bit younger than them), though she looked even younger than that. She'd been wandering round the Metro Centre on her own, and the girls let her tag along with them. Spuggie was OK but she could be a bit of a pest.

Donna pointed to a jacket in one of the shop windows. 'Hey, clock that! Fan-flippin'-tastic!'

'I bet your dad'll buy it for you,' said Spuggie enviously. Unlike Spuggie, who had nothing, Donna got everything she wanted.

High up on the Metro Centre roof, 'Gill' Gillespie and his sidekick Winston watched enviously as a bunch of leather-clad bikers roared around the open-air car park. Shiny black helmets and shades added to their air of menace. Gill, a big, good-looking boy with dirty blond hair, made a mental note to get himself a pair of shades. The mirror kind, where nobody could see your eyes. Well cool.

'Oy, you lot! Clear off! Or I'll have coppers on you!' The bikers just grinned, and deliberately rode close to the elderly attendant before zooming off down the ramp. Normally, Gill would have been the first to notice the pretty dark-haired girl, loaded down with boutique bags, who came out of the lift and walked past him. But he was too busy dreaming himself astride a gleaming black Harley Davidson.

Half an hour later, Gill and Winston were just finishing their Cokes in one of the shopping centre cafés as Donna, Nicola and Spuggie approached. Donna nudged Nicola and said loudly, 'Hey up, it's Gill and his pet monkey.'

Gill eyed them sardonically. These were two lippy females, though the Donna bird certainly went in and out in all the right places.

'You smell a funny pong, Win?' he said loudly. Winston grinned back. 'Yeah, a real pongy pong.' The pair of them sniffed the air exaggeratedly as they stood up and walked past the girls. 'Smells like daddy's been lashing out again.' Everybody knew that Donna's dad, landlord of the Byker Arms, spoiled his only daughter rotten. 'Hey, Bell's kid, what d'you call it, Eau de Brewery?'

'Drop dead,' said Donna and Nicola in bored unison.

'See you at the Grove later?' Gill grinned, not at all put out.

'Not if we see you first.' Donna and Nicola giggled at each other as they blew loud raspberries down their straws at the departing boys. They were going to the Grove anyway. That was their Saturday morning routine – a trip round the Metro Centre, then Byker Grove to find out what was on that night. Tonight one of the kids was having a birthday party.

'Can I come?' Spuggie asked – without much hope – as they walked along. She wasn't surprised when they said no. Anyway, she had nothing to wear.

Donna told them confidently that she was going with Cas Pearson. He was the best-looking boy at Byker Grove and she regarded him as her personal property.

'Why do you always call him Cas when his name's Andrew?' Spuggie wanted to know.

'Short for Casanova,' Donna giggled. 'Cos he's a right cute lover boy and he fancies me like mad.'

Nicola was used to Donna's showing off. She should be. They were best friends, after all. ''e fancies anything,' she said, then conceded, 'but he's all right, not like that yobbo Gill. I'd sooner snog with a gorilla.'

Donna stopped outside the cinema complex. 'I wouldn't mind seeing that,' she said. She and Nicola fixed up to go the following Tuesday.

'Can I come?' Spuggie asked again. Again she wasn't surprised when they said no. But she loved going to the pictures. This time she wasn't going to give up so easily.

Byker Grove was surrounded by large grounds, part of which had been converted into an adventure playground and a football pitch. Gill and Winston had already arrived by the time the three girls got there, and Gill was kicking a football around with some of the other lads.

Winston was off in a corner doing a deal with Cas Pearson. He'd brought a new dynamo for Cas's bike and Cas was objecting loudly to the price.

'This ain't junk, man, this is the business. For fifteen quid it's a giveaway, we're talking twenty to thirty in the shops. Minimum.'

'No chance,' said Cas.

'We can do a deal,' Winston replied.

'Watch it, Cas,' Nicola warned him. 'Winston's famous for his deals. The only one to get anything out of it is Winston.'

Donna linked her arm possessively through Cas's. 'I've got a great top for the party tonight,' she told him. 'You'll freak when you see it.' She really fancied Cas.

Inside the sprawling old house Donna and Nicola found the usual hive of activity. Alison Fletcher was supervising a cookery session in the kitchen. Alison was twenty-two, and a full-time assistant at the Grove. All the kids liked her, and the girls knew they could always go to her with their problems, though some of them thought she could look a lot prettier if she bothered with herself a bit more. She was showing a group of kids how to make Very Ginger Biscuits. Flour and treacle were everywhere.

In the large general room, other boys and girls lounged about discussing last night's rap concert, playing cards or Trivial Pursuit, and gossiping about their love lives. Over in the games room a couple of lads played table tennis while others lifted weights or worked out on the rowing machine. And in the quieter club room upstairs, two girls glumly tested each other on Macbeth for an exam.

Hayley Oduru, an attractive black girl of fifteen, was combing her hair in the girls' loo when Donna, Nicola and Spuggie walked in.

Spuggie decided there was no harm in trying just one more time. 'Why can't I come to the pictures with you?' she asked while Donna and Nicola primped in front of the mirror as usual.

'Because it's a flippin' fifteen, that's why, shrimp,' said Donna, spraying herself liberally with more of the yucky-smelling scent she'd bought earlier that morning.

'So? You're not fifteen,' said Spuggie, determined not to give up without a fight.

'No, but we look it. You look about six.' Nicola didn't mean to be unkind, but it was the truth. Everybody knew that. Even Spuggie. *Especially* Spuggie.

'I can look older. If you give me a lend of your eyeshadow and stuff.'

Nicola sighed. Spuggie could be a real pain at times. 'They'll not let you in, will you be told? Be dead embarrassing.'

Hayley felt sorry for the younger girl, with her freckled little face and usually cheeky grin. 'Why do you always call her Spuggie?' she asked.

'It's Geordie for sparrow, 'cos she's such a titch.' Donna added another coat of mascara to her already spiky eyelashes. 'Nearly thirteen and not even started growing boobs yet, have you Spug?' Donna eyed her own budding curves proudly in the mirror. 'Cas reckons I've got a great body. He says I'm going to be like Jamie Lee Curtis in another two years.'

The three older girls went out, leaving Spuggie looking hopelessly at herself in the mirror. She turned sideways on, and stuck her chest out as far as she could, but it was no use. Flat as a board. Blimmin' heck, surely there was *something* she could do? But she sighed as she realised that even if by some miracle she could make herself look older overnight, going to the pictures cost money. And, as usual, she was stony broke.

Donna and Nicola walked back to the Byker Arms, where Donna lived with her dad. As Donna let herself in, Mr Bell was hurrying through the hallway into the saloon bar to open up. Donna told him about the brilliant jacket she'd seen in the Metro Centre, and as she'd expected he said she could go back on Monday and buy it.

Donna was in a jubilant mood as she led Nicola upstairs to her bedroom – a mass of pink frills and cuddly toys. Donna had told Nicola she'd lend her something to wear to the party tonight, so Nicola wasted no time in going through her friend's overflowing wardrobe. Meanwhile Donna happily threw herself down on the pink satin bedspread and thought blissfully about the evening ahead, and herself, and Cas.

Unlike Donna, Julie Warner was sitting miserably in front of the TV in her parents' living room. She wasn't really watching the programme, she was more involved with her own unhappy situation. In the background her parents argued quietly. Her dad was still going on at her to try this stupid Byker Grove place but Mum was more understanding. She knew how Julie felt. All her *real* friends were at home in Wimbledon. Why should she try and get to know a whole bunch of strangers who even spoke differently to her?

'She doesn't want to go there because she's unhappy,' Mum was trying to explain to Dad. But it was no use. He said that was precisely why she *should* go to Byker Grove, to meet some young people of her own age.

'You can't just expect her to transplant herself as easily as that, Michael. She's at a sensitive age,' Mum told him.

Julie was fed up. 'I wish you'd both stop talking about me as though I wasn't here!' she flared.

Mr Warner sighed. 'We only want what's best for you, love.'

'Then you should have left me at home, shouldn't you? You shouldn't have made me come to this horrible dump in the first place!'

And with that she rushed tearfully out of the room, leaving Mr and Mrs Warner looking helplessly at each other.

On Monday after school, Gill and Winston were playing table tennis in the games room at Byker Grove when Spuggie came in. She'd been brooding on her problem ever since Saturday. 'I need to see you,' she told Winston urgently.

'Bog off, he's busy,' Gill scowled at her.

'I'm talking to Winston, not you.' Spuggie wasn't afraid of Gill, he was all talk. 'Haven't you got *any* jobs I could do?' she pleaded.

Business was business. In spite of Gill's obvious annoyance, Winston put his table tennis bat down, and brought out his personal organiser with a flourish. This, and the small moneybelt he always wore round his waist, were his trademarks. 'Doubt it. Not a lot of call for midgets.' Spuggie couldn't afford to take offence, her situation was too desperate. 'Please, Win!'

'There's babysitting, but you're too young for that,' he told her, flicking briskly through the pages. 'Same with paper round.'

But Spuggie wasn't going to be put off. 'There must be *something* I'm not too young for!'

'Yeah, weeding, but you'd be no good.'

'I can pull a few rotten dandelions out, piece of cake! Let me do it, Win. Go on, please.' Winston sighed and wrote down an address. Spuggie was jubilant as she tucked the grubby scrap of paper in her jeans pocket and left the lads to their game. 'Great! I'll go straight from school tomorrow!'

Meanwhile Hayley was just coming down the stairs as Rajeev Patel came into the Grove. Rajeev was a good-looking boy of nearly nineteen. He was also very bright and, like Hayley, very ambitious. He'd done his A levels the previous summer, and had spent some months on work experience in an electronics factory. Now he was helping temporarily in his father's corner shop, and was also a part-time volunteer worker at the Grove.

'When I've got my A levels I'm going to sit back and do flipping nothing for a bit,' Hayley told him, though secretly she admired the way Rajeev worked so hard towards the goals he'd set himself.

He grinned back at her. He'd made an agreement with his father. If he took a year off before going to university he'd spend some of it at home, helping out in the family business, and then he could travel. 'It's only

14

till July, then I'm off. India, the Far East, Australia, the lot. Me and me little backpack.'

Hayley regarded Rajeev as the older brother she'd never had. Like her, he came from a different background, and he understood her. He didn't say much, but he was always ready to listen. Though Hayley was only just fifteen, she already knew that most boys only wanted to talk about themselves. They weren't really interested in hearing about you or your problems.

Inside, in the general room, Gill was just lighting a cigarette when Geoff Keegan came in. Geoff ran the Grove like the captain of a ship. He was a chunky man, solidly built with plenty of muscle. Most of the time he was gentle and placid. You could take your troubles to Geoff. You also respected him. Nobody tangled with Geoff Keegan, not if they had any sense. But with a bug-eyed audience watching, Gill felt his macho reputation was at stake.

Geoff spoke quietly as he reached the table. 'Not in here, please Gill.'

Gill looked at him insolently. 'Can't see no sign.'

'We don't have written rules. It's a majority vote. As you well know.' Gill puffed defiantly on his cigarette. 'Either that goes out or you do.'

All the kids held their breath as Gill and Geoff looked at each other eyeball to eyeball. Gill was the first to look away.

'Ah, get stuffed,' he said, and sauntered out of the room, followed by his faithful acolyte Winston.

It was beginning to get dark as they walked down the path from the Grove into the adventure playground outside. Winston was silent. He was used to his friend's black moods. Gill slammed his fist into a tree trunk. 'It really chokes me off, being treated like a lousy kid.

That's me finished with that dump. Nowt to do there anyway.'

'Games room's not bad, Gill.' Winston rolled up his sleeve and proudly flexed his skinny arm muscles. 'I've put half an inch on there, easy.'

But Gill wasn't to be placated. 'There's other places to go, man. Real places that are mega cool. With music and strobes and lasers. And women.'

'They don't let you in them places at thirteen,' said Winston glumly.

'I'm fifteen.'

'Or fifteen.' Winston didn't care to argue with Gill normally, but it was getting cold. It was either going back into the Grove or going home. And he didn't much fancy going home right now. The dynamo he'd flogged to Cas was one he'd 'borrowed' off Eddie's bike. Eddie hardly ever used the bike, but with Winston's luck tonight he'd decide to go for a ride. Winston didn't mind that his family had to have a lodger, but he wished they could have found a smaller one, with a better temper.

Over in the far corner of the adventure playground Cas was optimistically trying to teach his dog to jump from the top of a wooden tower. 'It's not high, you stupid mutt!'

Popeye remained singularly unimpressed.

Winston grinned. 'You're not still trying to teach that fleabag tricks?'

'He's not a fleabag, he's one brilliant stunt dog, man!' Cas just knew Popeye had loads of potential. The only problem was, convincing Popeye.

The dog darted off up the path towards the Grove. 'Heel boy, heel, you know you're not allowed in there,' Cas yelled. 'Heel, you stupid pillock.' Popeye wagged his tail and disappeared through the front door. Cas shrugged philosophically, and followed the dog into the Grove. Winston watched them longingly.

'We going back as well, Gill?' he asked, shivering slightly in the chilly evening air. 'We could have a coffee. Or some pot noodles?'

'No way. I don't go nowhere to be treated like a piggin' kid. Nobody chucks Gill out.'

'He didn't chuck you out, he just said you couldn't smoke in there.'

But Gill was no longer listening. His attention had been caught by a girl of about fourteen who was getting out of a car. She'd be a right looker if she hadn't got that miserable expression on her face.

Mr Warner hated to see his daughter look so unhappy, but surely she couldn't be any more wretched at this Byker Grove place than she was at home. 'Go on then, love,' he said encouragingly, as she stood listlessly on the pavement. 'Pick you up about nine o'clock, all right?'

Without giving her time to change her mind, he drove off. Julie shrugged crossly. She remembered a puppy they'd found once. It had been friendless and abandoned. That's just how she felt. Oh, why did everything have to change?

'You look lost, girl.'

Julie jumped, slightly scared by this tall boy who suddenly loomed in her path, his torn leather bomber jacket painted with slogans, mouth unsmiling as he insolently eyed her up and down.

'I'm looking for Byker Grove.' Keep on walking, she told herself.

'Over there, behind them trees.'

'Right. Thank you very much.' Don't let him see you're scared, just keep on walking.

'Where you from then, Yorkie?' He had fallen into

step beside her. She stopped and took a deep breath. 'Wimbledon, actually.'

'That right?' A much smaller spiky-haired boy joined them, eyes gleaming with wicked mischief. 'Wimbledon Actually. She's from Wimbledon Actually.'

Winston and Gill usually got a good laugh out of their regular sport of winding girls up, but this time Winston was in for a disappointment, as Gill brusquely told him to belt up, and carried on questioning the newcomer. He found out that she'd recently moved to Northumberland with her parents because of her dad's job. And that she hated it.

'Don't you know any kids up here?'

'Not really. I've met a few in school. They're not really my type.'

'How about me? Reckon I'm your type, Yorkie?' His dark eyes were bold as they held hers in a challenging stare.

'Why d'you call me Yorkie?' She wanted to move on, but she couldn't. It was like those experiments in chemistry, when you held a magnet and all the iron filings were swept on to it. Except right now she felt like she was the iron filings.

He grinned disarmingly – no hint of menace now. 'Cos you talk like a blimmin' duchess. What d'you say your name was, anyway?'

'Julie.'

'I'm Gillespie. You can call me Gill. Brush 'ead here's Winston.'

Gill had evidently forgotten his earlier resolution not to go back to the Grove, as he walked along beside Julie. But the thought no longer gave Winston any pleasure, and he sulked along in their wake. Gill was his oppo, they were a team. He didn't like it when anybody else got in on their act. Especially not snooty birds from Wimbledon Actually.

In the games room, Cas was working out with weights when he saw something strange at the window.

'Gill, you nutter, what you doing?' he demanded, as Gill climbed nonchalantly over the sill into the room, followed by a somewhat reluctant Julie, and then a scowling Winston.

'Why do we have to come in this way?' Julie asked, puzzled, as Gill helped her into the room. Cas grinned at her as he cottoned on. As soon as he'd entered the Grove the ever-efficient jungle drums, with Spuggie as the chief drummer, had filled him in on the latest news. 'Cos Rambo here's had a spot of aggro with the guv'nor.'

'I can handle Geoff Keegan, don't you fret,' boasted Gill, as Cas eyed Julie with undisguised interest.

'What do they call you then, Blue Eyes?' he asked, smiling at her.

Gill grabbed her arm possessively. 'Her name's Julie, she's just moved here from Wimbledon,' he said.

'And I'm Cas,' long-lashed eyes smiled cheekily at her. Cas Pearson was a different kettle of fish altogether. Good-looking and lively, with bags of charm, he was an unashamed flirt.

Gill wasn't best pleased at any sign of muscling in on what he already regarded as his territory. 'Short for Casanova. You want to watch him,' he informed Julie, who had to hide a smile as she told him, 'I think I'm going to have to watch the lot of you!'

With both boys competing to show off their weight-lifting skills, Julie grudgingly began to suspect that this Grove place mightn't turn out to be so bad after all.

19

In the general room, Spuggie was shyly confiding to Hayley that her name was really Kirstie. 'That's pretty. Much prettier than Spuggie,' said Hayley.

'Oh, I don't mind. I don't mind being small. Everybody knows me. They've got a football team here and I'm the official mascot. I wouldn't be if I was big.'

But Hayley intuitively sensed something forlorn behind the younger girl's brave words. She looked up as a thin boy with a pale, intelligent face approached, to ask if Spuggie was being a pest.

'Oh, shove off, Fraser, who sent for you?' said Spuggie crossly. She and her brother had a constant love hate relationship. They were always sparring with each other, but woe betide any outsider who attacked either of them.

Fraser went back to his usual seat in the corner, and his pile of books, and Hayley wondered about this strange boy who seemed such a loner. Like Spuggie, he was always at the Grove, but unlike her he seldom mixed with the other kids. There was something about him that intrigued her. She couldn't help noticing that he hardly ever smiled, and that behind his specs his eyes looked older and sadder than his fourteen years.

Donna and Nicola were having a heated argument over the merits of George Michael versus Rick Astley when Nicola looked up and saw Gill in the doorway leading to the games room. 'Hey, Spuggie, go and tell Geoff that Gill's back,' she ordered. 'Go on, I dare you.' It was well known that Spuggie never refused a dare.

As Spuggie trotted off towards Geoff's office, Nicola prodded Donna gleefully. 'This should be good!' But Donna wasn't listening. She was staring across at the door where Gill and Cas were escorting a very flattered Julie into the room. Her eyes coldly swept the other girl up and down, and she didn't like what she saw, not one little bit. For one thing the girl was far too pretty. There was only room for one Beauty Queen Bee at Byker Grove – and that was Donna Bell. Also, Cas was gazing at her in a way which Donna definitely didn't like. But the final straw was the jacket. The same jacket that Donna had wanted so badly, but when she'd gone back to the shop in the Metro Centre the assistant said they'd sold the last one. And now this new girl was actually wearing it!

'Who the hell is she?' Donna hissed at Nicola. And as her gaze locked with Julie's, it was clearly a case of hate at first sight.

But before Donna's question could be answered, all eyes swivelled to the door as Geoff walked in, with round-eyed Spuggie hot on his heels. Julie was baffled when everyone fell silent. What on earth was going on?

'Calmed down, have you, Gill?' Geoff was smiling, very relaxed. Gill hadn't expected this laid-back approach. He didn't know how to deal with it. 'Wasn't me got me knickers in a twist, guv,' he said lamely.

'That's all right, then.' Geoff moved on. The room let out a collective sigh. Some were relieved, others disappointed, that there wasn't going to be a punch-up.

Donna watched narrow-eyed as Gill and Cas escorted Julie to the snack bar, and heaved a sigh of relief as they finally left her there with a cup of tea while they played a promised card game with two other lads.

As Julie stood uncertainly on her own, Hayley suggested that they should go over and say hello. 'What the heck for?' Donna demanded grimly. 'She's new, she doesn't know anybody,' Hayley explained. But Donna wasn't to be budged. In the end it was Alison who came to Julie's rescue. 'Hi, I'm Alison. I help Geoff run this place.'

'I'm not into youth clubs really,' Julie told her. In

spite of the boys' welcome, she still wasn't sure that she was going to like Byker Grove all that much. The three girls across the room all looked to be about her own age, but the attractive red-head with the frosty glare clearly wasn't about to put out the welcome mat.

Alison explained that the Grove was rather more than a youth club. It was really an alternative place to be. Somewhere you could go without any hassle from parents or teachers or other interfering grown-ups. 'Geoff and me are here, but we don't tell anybody what to do, that's mostly up to the kids themselves,' she said. She told Julie the Grove was open every day, and kids of all ages often came there straight from school. 'You can join in if you want, or just sit quietly upstairs in the club room and do your homework, or talk.'

As Alison talked, Julie was uncomfortably aware of the red-headed girl glaring at her with an expression that looked even less friendly than before.

'We have people who come in from outside to show us how to do various things, we're hoping to do photography soon, and we put on plays, discos, play all kinds of sport, outdoor activities. Have you seen anything of our local countryside yet, Julie?'

Julie shook her head. 'It's all dreary and ugly.'

'Blimmin' cheek!' the red-haired girl exploded.

'How do you know that?' Alison asked, with a funny little smile.

'When I told them at home that my dad's firm was moving him here, everybody said so,' Julie answered defiantly.

As Alison moved away, it was Spuggie who stepped shyly up to Julie. 'Your jacket's amazing, we saw it in the shop.' Julie looked at the small girl who was staring at her with a mixture of admiration and envy.

'Donna wanted it, didn't you, Donna?' Spuggie

22

added somewhat tactlessly. She was rewarded by a cuff on the head from Donna, and went back to the game of Monopoly she'd been playing with a couple of the other kids. If only some of this money was real she thought wistfully. Just a tiny *bit* of it . . . she sighed, and tried to concentrate on the game. Then she landed on Piccadilly but couldn't afford to buy it. Typical.

Donna stepped forward aggressively. She'd decided that attack was the best method of defence. Within seconds she'd learned Julie's age, name, and that she was only there because her dad's firm had moved him to the area.

'So what's he do then, your dad?' Julie began to resent the interrogation, as Donna stood in front of her gimlet-eyed.

'He works for a lighting company. He's a designer.' Stick that in your pipe and smoke it, she thought with satisfaction, but Donna only smirked smugly. 'My dad's self-employed.'

'He runs a pub,' Nicola mischievously interjected, and received a sharp dig in the ribs for her disloyalty. But Nicola couldn't care less. Donna might have been her best friend, but even best friends needed taking down a peg or two at times. Especially when they swanked as much as Donna did.

'What about your mum? I suppose she stops at home all day looking after her little precious.' Donna's voice had taken on an even more unpleasant tone, but Julie was too fed up to notice. Besides, the last thing she wanted was to talk about her parents to these strangers.

'Look, just leave me alone, will you? I don't have to answer your stupid questions, I didn't rotten well want to come here in the first place!'

'So who's asking you to stay then, blimmin' snob!'

By now, even Nicola had had enough of Donna's

spitefulness. 'Shut it, Donna,' she warned. Hayley tried to make peace, but her voice was drowned out as Donna yelled indignantly, 'Nicola Dobson can't tell me to shut it, gobby cow!'

Julie was close to tears. She'd become the centre of a row without even trying, and even Gill, her protector, seemed to be on the point of deserting her. 'Squawk squawk squawk!' Gill said, throwing his cards down onto the table. 'Squawking flippin' women,' he sneered, walking out of the room in disgust.

This was too much for Donna and Nicola. As usual they forgot their own quarrel as they united against Gill. 'Belt up, Gillespie!' they yelled in unison as he disappeared in the direction of the games room.

'Doesn't he have a first name?' Julie wondered aloud, to no one in particular. She was both scared and fascinated by this unexpected boy who could make her feel so special one moment, then act as if she didn't exist the next.

With Gill gone, she knew no one and another wave of loneliness and self-pity swept over her as she wandered out into the hallway.

A motherly-looking woman with grey hair was just coming in through the front door, a shopping basket on her arm. The woman peered into the office, but it was empty. 'Where's this place they call the snack bar then?' she demanded, fixing Julie with inquisitive eyes, and set off at a trot as Julie pointed the way.

Rajeev, who was on duty, was baffled when the elderly woman took a blackened soggy cake out of the basket on her arm. 'I made you a nice madeira,' she said, plonking it on the table. It made a dull thud as it hit the wooden top. Rajeev winced slightly. He had no idea who this strange apparition might be, nor what to do with her burnt offering. The mystery was unexpectedly solved by Nicola, as she hurled herself across the general room and into the snack bar. 'Gran, what the hell are you doing at the Grove?'

One of Nicola's main reasons for coming to the Grove, apart from the fact that it was a fun place to be, was to get away from Gran. The last thing she wanted was the nosy old biddy following her here. But Mary O'Malley needed something to fill her days now that she had moved in to live with her daughter's family and no longer had her own little place to run.

'You know I like to make myself useful, and watch your language, young lady.' Without pausing for breath, she carried on to an amused audience consisting now of Rajeev, Hayley and Donna.

'I can't be doing with just sitting on me bottom all day, never could, not even as a young person.' Mrs O'Malley peered into the general room. 'So this is where you spend all your time, is it?'

'Yes, Gran,' said Nicola in exasperation. 'Thanks for the cake, ta-ra.'

But Mrs O'Malley wasn't to be got rid of as easily as that. She was clearly bent on a further tour of inspection, with Nicola worriedly following in her tracks. Donna, grinning at her friend's embarrassment, tagged along too. Julie-whatever-her-name-was could wait.

'Hmmmmm.' Mrs O'Malley's eyes gleamed as she looked around the Grove's shabby old kitchen. Nicola watched apprehensively as she ran her finger along the grimy top of the ancient gas cooker. 'Bit of elbow grease on that'd do no harm, I might have a word with him as runs this place, and mind you're wearing a vest, our Nicola, it's a right biting wind they've got up here.'

Nicola fumed helplessly as Donna giggled infuriatingly. She wouldn't be seen dead wearing a rotten vest.

25

When Mrs O'Malley decided to explore upstairs, Nicola left her to it. She and Donna went back into the general room where Alison and Hayley were discussing the idea of a concert to raise some extra cash for the forthcoming camping trip.

Donna's eyes immediately lit up. 'Great, and I can do my Sue-Ellen, I'm brilliant at it, me dad says. And I can get the frocks off one of his girlfriends, she's a model, she's got tons of gear . . .'

Julie, standing hesitantly on the edge of the group, was puzzled. She turned to the girl they called Nicola, who seemed a lot less hostile than her friend. 'What does she mean, one of her dad's girlfriends?'

Nicola shrugged. 'He's got millions.'

Julie was even more shocked. 'Does her mother know?'

Taking her aside, Nicola explained that Donna's mum had run off with another man, leaving Donna with her dad. Jim Bell adored his only daughter, she was the apple of his eye. 'Spoils her rotten,' Nicola told Julie, without envy. 'Queen of the Byker Arms.'

Julie looked at her watch. The minute hand seemed to be crawling round. Even though Nicola and Hayley were including her in their conversation, she still felt she didn't belong here. She sighed. Right now she didn't feel she belonged anywhere. She'd said goodbye to all her friends in Wimbledon. She had to accept that was in the past. But what was in the present?

'Going already, Yorkie?' Gill had reappeared from the games room.

'In a few minutes.'

'Right then.' His tone was proprietorial as he took her arm. Julie felt a little thrill of pleasure tinged with apprehension.

'I don't actually need anyone to walk me home,

thank you . . .' she began, but Gill's smile had turned to a sneer. 'So who was offering, duchess?'

And before Julie could explain that her mum was picking her up in her car, he had swaggered out. As she stood there, blinking back sudden tears, the tall black girl approached and smiled. 'I'd keep away from him, pet,' she said gently.

But Julie felt too confused and emotional after the different events of the evening to respond to a friendly piece of advice. 'Oh, mind your own business and go back to where you came from, why don't you?' she was appalled to hear herself screaming. She saw the hurt flash in the girl's dark eyes, before she turned and abruptly walked away.

Mrs O'Malley had finished her tour of inspection. Just as she'd thought, there was plenty here to keep a body busy. She'd come back tomorrow and have a word with him as ran the place, she thought to herself as she walked down the drive. Then a muffled sobbing stopped her in her tracks. She followed the sound to some long grass on the edge of the playground. Spuggie was curled up in a tight, miserable little ball of tears.

'We can't have this. What's all this about then?' Mrs O'Malley was gentle under the brisk exterior.

'Nothing. I'm all right. Go away.' Spuggie wasn't in the mood to talk to anybody, least of all Nicola's nosy old granny.

But Mary O'Malley hadn't brought up a large family for nothing. 'You're about as all right as a chocolate tea-pot,' she pronounced, handing Spuggie a large clean hanky. 'What's up, eh lass?'

Spuggie sighed. She needed to tell somebody or she'd explode.

Sadly, she poured her heart out. She told Mrs

O'Malley how she hated being small, and never having any money. How much she envied girls like Donna Bell and the new girl, Julie, who wore such trendy clothes. How all the other kids would be going on the camping trip that Geoff was planning, but she knew without asking that she and Fraser wouldn't be able to.

'It's not fair. It's horrible being me, I wish I was dead. It's not fair . . .'

'Nay, you mustn't say that, lass.' Gran put her arms round Spuggie as she sobbed. 'It'll all work out, you'll see.'

Gill was seething as he and Winston took a short cut through a dingy alleyway.

'She's just a stupid stuck-up bird, Gill,' said Winston, who was secretly delighted that Julie had refused Gill's offer to walk her home. 'You're best off out.'

'You're right, Brush 'ead. Who needs her?' Gill's mood lightened as they approached the car park. Several motorbikes stood there, their sleek chassis gleaming invitingly in the light from the pub windows.

Gill and Winston prowled among them, longingly stroking a handlebar here, a headlamp there. Suddenly Gill straddled his legs across the saddle of a particularly hairy model. Winston looked at him in alarm.

'Hey, not that one man!'

'Why not? I'm pig sick of being told what I can't do. Let's have some action, we'll show the whole blimmin' lot of 'em, right?'

Winston took some persuading, but as usual Gill got his own way.

The Grove was about to close for the evening. Most of the kids had gone, and the few who remained were about to make their way home.

Rajeev unfastened the combination lock on his bike, and wheeled it down the path. He and Hayley usually walked part of the way together. He saw that her usually cheerful face looked tight and withdrawn, and knew that Julie's remark was still rankling.

'Don't let it bug you, kid.' He understood only too well how she was feeling. 'It's just ignorance. Besides, you were doing her a favour warning her off.'

Hayley had to smile in spite of her hurt. 'She certainly didn't see it that way.'

Rajeev grinned. 'Do girls ever, when somebody warns them off a lad?' They had reached the parting of the ways – Rajeev's father's corner shop.

'Good luck with your interview tomorrow.'

Hayley had confided to him that she was after a Saturday job as a chambermaid in a small private hotel. Her mum was unable to work because she had chronic arthritis, and they needed the extra money.

'Thanks. Keep your fingers crossed that they don't find out I'm only fifteen. See you, Raj.'

Rajeev unlocked the side door to the living accommodation above the shop, as Hayley walked on into the night. He knew she didn't have an easy time of it, with her sick mother and no one else to turn to. But Hayley was strong, proud and determined, as well as being very bright. If anybody could overcome all the obstacles in her path, she could.

Back at the Grove, Geoff and Alison were finishing some paperwork when Geoff paused, looking puzzled. 'I thought you said they'd all gone?' A tiny, repetitive clicking sound was coming from the games room.

Geoff opened the door to find Spuggie alone in the darkened room, moodily bouncing a ping pong ball on the table.

'Spuggie? Home time. Everybody else has gone.'

'All right.'

As Geoff walked back into the general room, Alison asked him if Spuggie was all right. 'She seemed a bit quiet earlier. Not our usual bouncy wee lass.'

'Have you noticed,' Geoff said thoughtfully, 'that she and Fraser are always the last to go home?'

'How was it, sweetheart?' Mrs Warner asked anxiously as Julie sat silently in the car next to her. She wasn't encouraged by her subdued reply, 'All right.'

'Will you go again?'

'Dunno.' Suddenly Julie sat up and peered out of the car window as they drove past a piece of wasteland.

'Mum! Stop a minute!'

A strangely familiar figure sat astride a large, powerful-looking motorbike. Julie stared in horrified fascination as she recognised Gill.

Winston, who had 'borrowed' a much smaller model, was cautiously going round and round in circles, but as Gill caught sight of Julie watching him, he decided to show her that she wasn't dealing with any stupid little kid.

Vroom, vroom! He revved the powerful engine up and roared past her.

'We've got to get back, love,' Mrs Warner said, driving on. She had no idea that Julie had any connection with the yobs on the bikes.

Gill, still showing off and thinking of the leather-clad bikers he'd watched so enviously at the Metro Centre last Saturday, zoomed straight at Winston.

'Hey man! First one to swerve's chicken!' he yelled, high on anger, exhilaration and the thrill of danger.

Winston's eyes widened in stark terror as the monster bike came straight at him.

CHAPTER TWO

Gill found himself sprawled in a patch of slimy mud. Painfully he picked himself up and winced as his foot touched the ground. His ankle hurt like mad but he didn't think it was broken. Near him lay the once proud monster of a bike, its paintwork scratched, bumper dented and headlamp smashed. He ran an experimental tongue round his mouth, hoping he hadn't knocked out any teeth.

Wiping his face on his sleeve, he gingerly made his way over to a small hump on the ground a few metres away. Winston lay spreadeagled and motionless, his 'borrowed' motorbike nearby, slightly damaged but with its engine still running. 'Winston?' The hump didn't move. 'Win? You all right, man?' But Winston remained motionless. Gill felt the first stirrings of panic. Tentatively he bent down towards the immobile form. Where the heck was the pulse supposed to be? They'd had a first aid course at the Grove last year, he wished he hadn't dismissed it as strictly for wallies. Should he try the kiss of life? He didn't much fancy it. Blimmin' heck, if anybody passed and saw him. . . . Still, old Win did look in a pretty bad way.

'Win? Speak to me, man. You OK?'

'Stupid piggin' question.' Winston started to sit up, hesitantly feeling his arms and legs for broken bones.

'Here.' Relieved, Gill held out a helping hand as Winston attempted to stand. But Win pushed it brusquely away.

'Thanks for nothing, man!' he called over his shoulder angrily, as he hobbled off into the night.

Gill stood there, not sure what to do next. He was trying to right one of the bikes when he heard voices. As he started to run, a sharp twinge of pain shot through his left ankle. Cursing, he limped as fast as he could towards the safety of home.

But he wasn't going to get away with it as easily as that. The next afternoon, as Gill limped along a back alley on his way to the Grove, the sound of motorbikes shattered the silence behind him. He felt the hair on the nape of his neck prickle in alarm as two helmeted, leather-jacketed figures roared up closer on either side of him. One of the bikers dismounted and grabbed Gill by the collar. When he spoke his voice was as coldly menacing as his appearance. 'Next time you lay a finger on anybody's flaming bike you'll end up with a lot more than a limp, sunshine,' he snarled. 'And that's a promise.'

The two bikers roared off as suddenly as they'd appeared, leaving a very shaken Gill.

It was a bright sunny afternoon. Snowdrops and crocuses pushed their heads up through the ground, and fluffy cottonwool clouds scudded across a pale blue sky. Spuggie skipped along, the previous night's black mood completely swept away at the thought of all the money she was going to make. How much would she get for pulling out weeds? A quid? Two? Five, even? Five pounds. Lost in a blissful daydream about what she might do with such untold wealth, she nearly tripped over a small dog that ran barking across the path.

'He'll not bite you, hinny,' said an old man who was stooping over in an allotment planting seedlings in neat rows. He introduced himself as Mr Pimlott, and said his dog was called Tinker.

'I'm Spuggie,' she said, patting Tinker, and proudly

told Mr Pimlott that she was off to weed another allot-ment further up the lane.

'Oh aye? Which one'll that be?' asked Mr Pimlott, with a kindly smile.

Spuggie consulted the scrap of paper Winston had given her. 'Number 39.'

'Not old Ben Stewart's?' He'd stopped smiling now.

'Must be, if that's number 39,' she replied, wonder-ing why Mr Pimlott was suddenly looking at her so peculiarly.

Spuggie ran eagerly on her way, and then skidded to a disbelieving halt. She looked back at Mr Pimlott, keeping her fingers crossed that he'd tell her she'd made a horrible mistake – that this wasn't number 39. But he nodded his head glumly, and a crudely painted number on the ramshackle fence confirmed her worst fears. The entire allotment was covered in nettles, brambles and horsetails almost as tall as Spuggie herself. She nearly turned and ran there and then . . . until she remembered the pictures, and how much she wanted to go with Donna and Nicola that night. Sigh-ing, she took off her anorak, rolled it up in a bundle, and opened the rickety wooden gate.

On his way to the Grove, Geoff frowned as he saw Gill lounging about outside.

'Gill?'

Gill jerked his head towards the Grove. 'Blimmin' door's locked.'

'It will be. We don't open until four.' Geoff glanced suspiciously at his watch, obviously assuming Gill had bunked off school. Gill airily informed him that it was games last lesson, and he couldn't be bothered going.

Geoff was sceptical, but gave him the benefit of the

doubt. As Gill walked away, Geoff noticed his limp. He shrugged as he unlocked the front door of the big old house – what Gillespie did outside Byker Grove was his own business.

There was a pile of letters waiting on the mat and Geoff sorted through them quickly as he went into the office. He stopped at one bulky little package, and scanned the name and address on the jiffy bag. 'Fraser Campbell, c/o Byker Grove, Byker Park, Newcastle-Upon-Tyne.' Puzzled, Geoff put the package on the desk. Then he set about the daily routine of the Grove, making a note to talk to Alison about where they were planning to take the kids for the camping trip in May.

An hour later, and the Grove was buzzing. Cas and Brian, otherwise known as Speedy, were playing Trivial Pursuit in the general room. Cas was winning by a mile, but then he usually did. General knowledge was not one of Speedy's strong points. Absorbed in the game, neither of the boys looked up when a weary Spuggie limped in, her hands grimy and covered in scratches. 'Is Winston here yet?'

Cas shook his head. 'Not seen him.' He threw the dice as Gill wandered in, trying to appear unconcerned. Spuggie dashed over to him. 'Have you seen Winston?'

Gill looked scared. Did the little squirt know something he didn't? 'No. Why, what's happened to him?' he asked apprehensively and was relieved when Spuggie explained that Winston owed her some money.

Still, perhaps he should go and make sure Brush 'ead was OK. Sighing with the unfairness of it all, he limped out of the door, his sprained ankle still hurting. All he'd wanted was a bit of fun, surely he didn't deserve all this aggro?

Mrs Warner stopped the car just short of the entrance to Byker Grove.

'Are you sure you want to go, Julie?' she asked sympathetically, seeing Julie's glum expression. 'You don't have to.'

Julie shrugged, and got out of the car.

Mrs Warner sighed. Julie wasn't making it easy, but then things weren't easy for any of them. 'See you later, love. Have a good time,' she called as she drove away.

Julie didn't think there was much chance of that, if yesterday was anything to go by. But anything was better than sitting at home, with Mum and Dad both on edge all the time. And she did feel bad about what she'd said to Hayley, she had to put that right somehow.

Cas and Speedy were still playing Trivial Pursuit in the general room, with Spuggie constantly chipping in, when Julie arrived. Cas threw her a flirtatious smile. 'Hi there, Julie,' he called, and introduced her to Speedy. 'Julie's new here, she doesn't know anybody.'

'I didn't know nobody neither when I first come,' Speedy told her.

Julie was instantly sympathetic. 'Did your family have to move too?'

'Got no family. I'm fostered,' he said matter-of-factly. 'Before that I was in a home.' Brian Clark wasn't a home-grown Geordie like the rest of them. He was a Lancashire lad whose mum had had to hand him over to the social services when he was five, but he never moaned about his lot. Good at sports, placid and always ready to do a mate a favour, Brian was popular among the kids. Even if he had been nicknamed Speedy because he wasn't exactly the brightest of boys.

The two lads went off to play table tennis, and Julie was grateful that at least *they* made her feel welcome. Just as she was asking Spuggie if she'd seen Hayley,

Donna arrived. 'Oh aye, Lady Muck's back,' said Donna in a loud voice.

Julie wasn't miffed, she was getting used to Donna by now. 'I came to see Hayley, not that it's anything to do with you.'

Donna grinned knowingly at Nicola. 'I don't suppose it's anything to do with Gorgeous Gillespie either. Just saw him in the street if you're interested.'

'I'm not,' said Julie, turning a tell-tale shade of scarlet.

Spuggie chipped in eagerly, 'Was Winston with him?' Blimmin' heck, she'd worked hard enough on those dratted weeds. Now she wanted her dosh.

Nicola was surprised that Julie had turned up again. None of them had thought she'd come back to the Grove. But as she saw Julie's eyes flicker hopefully to the door each time someone new came in, Nicola realised that for once Donna was right. It was Gill she'd come to see. Well, good luck to her – it certainly took all sorts. Not that Gill didn't have a certain sexy charm. But he was dangerous and moody – neither of them qualities that Nicola prized in a man. When she fell in love she wanted him to be someone dead romantic – not wimpy but gentle. Someone who'd bring her red roses and tell her she looked like Kim Wilde.

Nicola snapped out of her daydream when Spuggie, always glad to be the bearer of bad tidings, said gleefully, 'I've got some news for you.'

'Oh yes?' said Nicola, bored. She was used to Spuggie's news items.

'Your gran's here. She's cleaning the kitchen.'

'Oh no!' wailed Nicola, as she dashed from the room.

Geoff was helping some kids paint a mural on the large wall outside when Nicola raced up to him, furious that he'd given Mrs O'Malley the job of regular helper.

At supper last night when Gran had threatened to

offer her services at the Grove, Nicola had warned her in no uncertain terms to keep away. But it was becoming increasingly clear that Nicola wasn't the only member of the family with a mind of her own.

'I told her we couldn't afford to pay her but she said she just wanted to keep busy,' Geoff explained.

Nicola was not to be appeased. 'Yeah, busy poking her nose in my blimmin' business,' she stormed.

'She only wants to help,' Geoff said mildly.

'You could have said no!'

'Have you tried saying no to your gran?' Geoff asked with a grin, attempting to soothe her by saying that maybe Mrs O'Malley would soon get fed up with the rowdy Byker Grovers. But Nicola just stalked disgustedly back into the house.

None of her friends would have recognised Hayley, as she walked along the waterfront. She wore a neat suit with a blouse tied in a bow at the neck, and matching court shoes. It was an outfit she'd borrowed from her mum, because she didn't want to go for a job interview looking like a schoolgirl. They'd both giggled at her strange appearance, and then her mum had looked sad, as she told Hayley how much she wished she didn't have to take on this extra burden. Hayley had enough to do already with all her schoolwork. GCSEs were coming up, and Hayley was determined to get brilliant results.

'If only I could go back to work. . .' her mother had sighed.

'You will. The doctor said. Until then we've agreed, I'll get a Saturday job and help out. Me and me magic broom.' Hayley spoke in a tone of finality, and Mrs Oduru knew that once her stubborn daughter made her mind up there was no point in arguing.

Now, a familiar voice called 'Hi!', and Hayley saw Rajeev loading some boxes into his father's van. She told him she'd had her interview, and that she could start on Saturday.

'Great. Terrific. Congratulations.' Hayley felt his response was a bit over the top. 'Raj,' she said drily, 'I'll be a glorified chambermaid-cum-char, not the next Prime Minister!'

But Rajeev was unabashed. 'I dunno. You *look* like the next Prime Minister in that get-up.' He smiled. 'Anyway, you've got the job with no hassle about your age, so why are you looking so miserable? I thought it was what you wanted?'

'We could use the money, that's for sure, but it's yet another commitment,' she sighed. 'Raj, I know I'm bright, I'm not being big-headed. They all say I'll go on to university.'

'You will,' he said with conviction. Rajeev had had his future mapped out since he was about five and somebody had bought him a starter electronics kit. He planned to do a degree in electronic engineering.

Hayley wished she shared his utter certainty. She told him how her mum had never been married, her dad had split when Hayley was a baby, and Ruth had done a terrific job of bringing her daughter up on her own. 'She used to work till she got arthritis. *She's* bright too, my mum, but she never had the breaks. She wants it to be better for me. I always thought that's what I wanted. This great career.'

Rajeev smiled. 'You're not thinking of quitting school, getting married and having half a dozen kids instead?'

'No way!'

'Or working in a supermarket?'

Hayley had to smile as she explained that the problem was that everyone expected so much of her. Her school, her mum, even the people at the Grove. 'You'll cope, Hayley,' they said. Part of her responded to the challenge, but another part of her felt like running away to a desert island and not having to prove anything to anybody.

Rajeev took her hand sympathetically to show that he understood and she smiled at him gratefully. It was so *good* just to have someone to talk to sometimes. People didn't seem to realise how important it was to get these complicated feelings off your chest. Being fifteen, and a girl, and black, and ambitious, that was quite some weight to carry.

In the office at Byker Grove, Geoff and Alison were speculating on the package that had arrived earlier. 'Whatever it is, why would Fraser have it sent here instead of to his home?' Alison asked.

Geoff was just as puzzled – and concerned. 'I don't know, but I'm sure there's something really bothering that lad,' he said, though he felt it was best not to push it at this stage. After all, if any of the kids had a problem, they usually came to him or Alison in their own good time.

They both looked up as they heard footsteps in the hall and Jim Bell appeared in the office doorway. The two men knew each other well, Geoff frequently popped into the Byker Arms for a quick pint before going home. But Jim wasn't wearing his usual affable smile, and he closed the door behind him as he came into the room – a sure sign that this wasn't a social call.

He told them that two motorbikes had been pinched from the pub car park the previous night. They'd been found later, damaged, on a nearby croft. 'Obviously kids joyriding,' Jim said, and reluctantly added that he was worried that some of the Byker Grovers might have been responsible. Geoff knew it was more than a possibility. 'They're not all angels, by any means,' he admitted.

'Keep your ears open, mate. If you do get a sniff it's kids who come here, let 'em know they won't be so lucky next time. *I'll* call the cops in if nobody else does. I don't want the Byker Arms getting known as a place that's not safe to leave your transport.'

Geoff promised Jim he'd bear it in mind, and showed him to the door. But outside in the hallway more trouble was waiting, in the furious shape of Donna. Angrily she hurled herself at her dad, as Nicola and Spuggie hovered nosily in the background.

'Dad! You're horrible! You promised!' Donna accused. Jim had told her earlier on that he was going to have a word with Geoff about the stolen bikes, and the last thing she wanted was to look a prat in front of her mates. 'I'll look well stupid if you go flinging accusations about all over the show,' she had said angrily.

But much as he adored his daughter, Jim had the good name of his pub to think of. 'I've got a business to run, sweetheart,' he said now. 'Besides, if everybody's behaved themselves, nobody's got anything to worry about, have they?'

He tried to kiss her cheek, but Donna sulkily turned her head away and went back into the general room, followed by Nicola and Spuggie.

A few minutes later, it was Nicola's turn to look cross as Mrs O'Malley came out of the kitchen.

'Shining like a new pin in there,' she said with satisfaction.

'Good,' said Nicola. 'Then it won't want doing for another six months.' But her satisfaction was shortlived. Gran informed her that she planned to come in every day, and she was going to tackle Geoffrey's pigsty of an office next time. In the same breath she asked Nicola what was that stuff on her eyes.

'It's eyeshadow, Gran. Frosted coffee bean,' Nicola said through clenched teeth.

'Looks like dirty marks to me. We never used to put stuff on our eyes when we was your age, a young skin doesn't need all that expensive muck,' Gran said, and satisfied that she'd had the last word she swept out of the room, leaving Nicola seething.

In the hallway Mrs O'Malley bumped into Spuggie, and asked her if she was feeling any better today.

'A bit,' Spuggie said, then confided that she was going to the pictures that night. 'If I've got enough money. And if I can make myself look older. And if they'll take me with them,' she added.

Gran took two ten-pence pieces from her purse and furtively slid them into Spuggie's hand. 'There, put that towards it. You can tell me all about it tomorrow.'

Spuggie looked happily at the two coins, then put them carefully into her purse, before going into the general room with Hayley, who had just arrived.

As Julie saw Hayley come in at last she crossed over to her. 'Could I have a word?' she asked hesitantly.

Hayley's response wasn't encouraging. 'I'm busy,' she said coolly, turning away. Julie couldn't blame her for reacting like that, and took it in good part. 'Please, Hayley,' she said, and the other girl relented slightly as she followed Julie over to a quiet corner.

'Go ahead.' Hayley's tone was still far from friendly.

Wishing once again that she were a million miles away from this place, where she seemed to get into trouble every time she opened her mouth, Julie apologised to the other girl. 'I shouldn't have said what

41

I did. About going back to where you came from. I'm sorry,' she said.

Hayley looked her in the eye. 'Yeah, well, p'raps you'll think twice before making nasty remarks in future.' But Julie sensed with relief that her apology had been accepted, and that Hayley wasn't the type to hold a grudge.

At least she'd sorted that out. But there was still no sign of Gill. She wasn't sure why she wanted to see him again so much. She just knew she did – and that there were questions she had to ask.

Gill had taken himself off to find Winston. He was pretty certain the kid was OK, but he reckoned he'd better make sure. At Winston's house, his gran told Gill he'd probably be at the Monument, a well-known Newcastle landmark and a popular rendezvous for all the local kids.

Sure enough, Gill found Winston at the Monument, talking to Speedy. Gill limped over to them. 'So you're OK?' he said, trying to sound nonchalant.

'No thanks to you,' Win replied angrily. 'You're a pigging maniac, man. You want locking up, you do!'

Gill glared at him to shut up, he didn't want it broadcasting. But it was too late, Winston had already told Speedy the whole story.

'You're a right nutter, Gillespie,' Speedy said.

Gill was in no mood to be ticked off, and certainly not by that dope Clark. 'Listen who's calling me,' he sneered. 'Wally Thicko, whose idea of a big thrill's sneaking into St James's Park for free.' St James's Park was the local football ground, home of Newcastle United (commonly known as the Magpies because of the black and white strip they wore).

Speedy wasn't in the least ruffled. 'At least I won't end up dead,' he said.

'I've got news for you, sunshine,' retorted Gill. 'We all end up that way.' And he limped slowly back in the direction of the Grove, with the other two boys following behind.

As Fraser walked past the office on his way to the general room, Geoff called him in, and gave him the package. 'This came for you.'

'What is it?' Fraser asked nervously. The boy looked permanently anxious, thought Geoff, as if he was always poised on the edge of some catastrophe waiting to happen. 'There's nothing bothering you, lad, is there?' he asked, as Fraser stood there with the package in his hands.

'No.'

Geoff sighed. Communicating with Fraser was like drawing teeth. 'Only if there is, you know we're here. Always ready to listen.'

Fraser remained silent and Geoff gave up for the time being. No use pushing the boy. 'Aren't you going to open it?' he asked, handing Fraser some scissors. Carefully, his face unsmiling, Fraser slit the wrapping, as if expecting something nasty to emerge. Then he gasped in sheer astonishment.

Inside the package was a brand-new wristwatch. Digital, shockproof, waterproof, it told the date and was a calculator as well. For once Fraser's face was really animated as he examined it and excitedly handed it to Geoff to look at. Then he showed Geoff the letter that came with it. He had entered a competition in a computer magazine, and the letter said he'd won a runners-up prize.

'Well done, Fraser,' Geoff congratulated him

warmly. 'By heck, it's a canny watch is that.' Then, as he handed it back, he asked casually, 'Not that I mind, but why did you put the Grove's address on the entry form, lad?'

Fraser shrugged the question off, saying, 'Oh, you know what they're like at home, always wanting to know everything.'

'I should have thought you'd want them to know. Not everybody can win a belting prize like that,' Geoff commented. Fraser didn't reply, but to Geoff's further surprise, put the watch in his pocket.

'Are you not going to wear it?' Geoff couldn't help asking.

'No.' The boy hesitated. 'And Geoff . . . I'd be glad if you didn't tell nobody.

'Not even Spuggie?'

'Especially don't tell Spuggie. Please?'

'If you say so, lad,' Geoff concurred, and as Fraser left the office, found himself more puzzled than ever.

In the general room, Spuggie was still keeping her eyes glued to the door, waiting for Winston. Usually he was one of the first to turn up. He *would* be late today when she desperately needed to see him. Typical. She scowled when Fraser came over and asked how the weeding had gone.

'Rotten,' she said, 'and what's so funny?'

'Nothing.'

'So why are you smiling?' she asked suspiciously. Fraser seldom smiled. If he was laughing at her, she'd flipping well kick him on the shins for his cheek. Fraser sunnily repeated that he wasn't smiling at anything special, but Spuggie wasn't satisfied with that. 'Secrets!' she called after him, as he went over to his usual corner. 'You've always got blimmin' secrets. Right, I shan't tell you anything now!'

'Good,' said Fraser infuriatingly, as he buried his nose in one of his books, still with that silly grin all over his stupid face.

At the snack bar, Hayley and Julie were getting to know one another much better, and to their surprise they discovered they had quite a lot in common. Julie wasn't sure that she should be telling anyone about her family problems – but she instinctively felt she could trust Hayley, who was only a few months older than she was but seemed so grown-up. She told Hayley how nothing was the same at home any more – and how unhappy her mum had been since they'd moved to Newcastle. 'She hates being stuck at home all day, she had a good job before.'

'My mum's stuck at home all day too,' Hayley sighed, as she explained how Ruth Oduru's illness had forced her to give up work. But even though there were only the two of them, they managed pretty well. 'The main thing is we get on great, she's more like a sister than a mum.'

'I always wanted a sister,' Julie said wistfully. 'I'm an only child.'

'Yeah, me too.'

As they shared confidences, each girl began to feel she had made a new friend. Then, out of the corner of her eye, Julie saw Gill come in, but he paid her no attention as he went over to the snack bar and bought a bag of crisps. Only then did he walk casually over to Julie. He'd deliberately not gone up to her straight away. It didn't do to look too keen. Where birds were concerned, a laid-back approach was best. Play it cool, that was the way.

'So, you came back then, Yorkie,' he commented, offering her a cheese and onion crisp.

Julie tried to match his casualness. 'There's not

much else to do round here.' Then, even though she suspected it would make him angry, she had to ask the question which had been troubling her. 'What on earth were you doing last night? Whose motorbike was that?'

He wasn't angry, he seemed almost proud of himself as he shushed her with a wink. 'Our secret, eh? Wouldn't want to get a pal in bother, would you?' He clearly had no intention of explaining himself further, so Julie asked about his family, thinking it might help her to understand him better. 'What are your mum and dad like?' she asked innocently. But his eyes were suddenly like chips of ice as he said coldly, 'You ask a lot of questions, duchess,' and moved away to where Speedy and Cas were playing dominoes.

Julie sighed, wondering what she'd done wrong this time. She wasn't to know that Gill's mother was a warm-hearted but feckless woman who spent most of her day in a cluttered, untidy room watching soaps on the telly, while his dad was almost permanently in jail. Julie would have been astounded if she'd realised the enormous difference there was between her own usually comfortable, well-ordered home life and the permanent chaos of Gill's.

Across the room, Spuggie saw Winston finally come in, and dashed over to him. 'Hey, you, you owe me some money,' she demanded. But Winston said there was nothing doing – she'd get no money till she'd finished the job.

'I'm not going to, Mr Pimlott says you'd need a bulldozer to shift that lot. I still want paying for what I did, it was blimmin' hard work. Look.' She held out her scratched and blistered hands.

Winston tried to tell her he'd have to get it from 'his client' first, but Spuggie wasn't to be fobbed off. She needed the money *now*, they were going to the pictures *tonight*. Sighing, Winston took a coin from his moneybelt.

'Fifty pence?' said Spuggie, outraged. 'Fifty lousy rotten pence for all that work?'

'My commission's got to come out of it,' said Winston grandly. 'Take it or leave it.'

Spuggie tipped out of her purse the other coins she'd carefully hoarded over the past few weeks and did a quick calculation. Together with Mrs O'Malley's contribution and the fifty pence, she'd just have enough to buy a ticket. There'd be nothing left over for sweets or an ice-cream, but at least she could go with the others and see the film . . . 'Give it here,' she sighed, and took the coin, giving Winston a dirty look. Talk about blimmin' slave labour!

At this point, Geoff came in and immediately registered Winston's battered appearance. 'Had an accident, Winston?' he asked casually. Winston mumbled some sob story about having fallen out of a tree while rescuing a poor old lady's cat. But Geoff had now turned his attention to Gill. 'And I noticed you were limping,' he remarked, deceptively relaxed.

Gill shrugged. 'Games last lesson,' he said. 'Some clown tripped me.'

Geoff eyed them both up and down. He seemed to grow taller before their eyes as he said, 'OK, sunshine.' He nodded to Winston. 'And you. I know what you've both been up to.'

Around them, the room fell silent. The kids at Byker Grove had antennae like bats when it came to scenting trouble. And this looked like trouble with a capital T.

'Ain't been up to nothing, Geoff, honest,' whined Winston.

But Geoff wasn't fooled. 'Do I look stupid, lad?' he asked. Both Gill and Winston knew better than to answer this. 'So you reckon it's clever stuff, joy-riding on stolen motorbikes. Shows you're real big shots, right?' His tone hardened. 'Wrong. What it shows is you're a right pair of wallies. Nobody's impressed. I'm not. I can tell you the blokes whose bikes you nicked certainly weren't. You're damn lucky they didn't fetch the police in.' He eyed them both contemptuously. 'You're damn lucky you're alive. Next time you mightn't be. And if you do live to tell the tale, you'll not be telling it in here, that's for sure. Because you'll be banned.' Aware that every eye was on him, he turned to the other kids, and spoke with steely authority. 'And that applies to anybody else who gets any clever ideas, all right?' There was a stunned silence as Geoff left the room, followed by Gill and Winston a few moments later.

Julie looked helplessly across at Hayley, who shrugged as if to say, 'I told you so.' Hayley wouldn't trust Gill as far as she could throw him.

'Why on earth would he do a crazy thing like that?' Julie asked.

It was Nicola who answered. 'Takes after his old man, doesn't he? He's in the nick more often than he's out.'

'How do you know that?' Julie was both scared and intrigued by this glimpse of a world so different to her own.

'My flippin' gran, she knows everything. Me dad calls her the eyes and ears of the world. Why are you so interested, pet?' Nicola asked, but not nastily.

Julie was genuinely confused. 'I don't know. I've never met anybody like him before,' she said. Then broke off in astonishment. 'Good grief!'

The other girls followed her gaze to the doorway, where a weird sight met their eyes. Spuggie had spent the best part of an hour in the girls' loo trying to make herself look older. She'd cadged some make-up from one of the older girls, and her little face was plastered with eyeshadow, blusher and bright pink lipstick. Wads of loo roll were stuffed down the front of her T-shirt to give her some 'boobs', and as she tottered over to Donna on borrowed high heels that were much too large, there was a smug grin on her face. She'd got the cash, she looked fifteen, she'd cracked it. They couldn't refuse to take her now!

'Take you where? asked Donna blankly.

'The pictures. You said you were going tonight.'

'Sorry, Spug.' Donna was dismissive. 'Didn't we mention, we're not bothering. Fiona saw it and said it was yuck.'

It was all Spuggie could do to hold back the tears. She fumbled down the front of her T-shirt for some loo roll, and defiantly blew her nose. She wasn't going to cry in front of them. No way were they going to call her a stupid kid. No way. She turned and fled from the room.

Speedy was just leaning his bike up against the wall outside the Grove when Gill came hurtling out, closely followed by Winston.

'Had to go and grass on us, didn't you?' he roared at an astonished Speedy. 'Stitched me up proper. Thanks for nothing, mate.' Then he snarled at Winston, 'I told you you were daft to trust him!'

But even as Speedy was protesting his innocence, Gill was calling him a lying pig, and lashing out with all his considerable strength. Speedy, no slouch either in that department, automatically defended himself. His bike fell over with a crash and Cas's dog Popeye, tied to a railing, barked with frustrated excitement, wanting to join in the fray.

On the point of going home, a tearful Spuggie soon

forgot her own disappointment when she saw the flying fists. She turned and ran back into the Grove to get Geoff. He came out and quickly separated the protagonists, who stood panting and glaring as the other kids, alerted to a punch-up, came running out of the front door.

'Right. That's enough of that. What's going on?' demanded Geoff.

Both Gill and Speedy remained silent. Geoff wasn't about to let it go at that. 'Gill?' he said. Then, 'Speedy?'

Feeling the need to declare his innocence, Speedy blurted out that he'd not said anything to Geoff. Gill, not believing him, called him a flaming nark.

That was when Geoff stepped in. He coolly informed Gill that it wasn't Speedy or anyone else who had dropped him in it. It was his own stupidity. He'd told Geoff that he'd hurt his leg when some clown had tripped him at games. 'But you didn't go to games, Gill. You told me you bunked off. Or had you forgotten?'

Gill's face was reply enough. He looked both sheepish and embarrassed, while he cursed himself inwardly. Keegan was too blimmin' sharp. Next time he fed him a line, he'd have to remember to cover his tracks better.

Geoff went back inside, and most of the other kids straggled back in after him. The fun was obviously over. Only Gill, Julie, Speedy and Winston remained. Silently Julie handed Gill a hanky to wipe his bloodied nose. Winston tentatively asked him if he was OK.

'It's the other feller you want to worry about,' said Gill, quickly recovering some of his usual swagger.

'Nowt wrong with me, Charlie,' said Speedy. 'If Geoff hadn't come you'd have been begging for mercy.'

'Yeah, you and whose army?' retorted Gill. But the heat had gone out of their dispute, and they grinned through bruised lips at each other as Cas and Donna came out of the Grove and said they were going for chips.

'Tell you what, scrapping doesn't half give you an appetite,' Gill announced. 'Anybody fancy joining 'em? Brush 'ead? Speed?'

Both Winston and Speedy recognised an olive branch when it was waved under their noses.

'My treat,' Gill added grandly, then turned to Julie. 'How about you, Yorkie?'

But Julie reluctantly had to explain that she couldn't, she had to go home. As Cas, Donna, Winston and Speedy walked ahead, Gill lingered. 'See you tomorrow?' he asked.

Julie smiled shyly, with just a hint of flirtatiousness. 'If you like,' she said. Then, as he was about to follow the others, she stopped him. 'Here. You've still got some blood on your nose.' Taking the hanky from him, Julie gently cleaned up Gill's face.

Suddenly a car drew up alongside them, and Julie's mother stared aghast as her daughter tenderly wiped blood and dirt off the face of a yobbo in a torn leather jacket.

'Julie!' she cried, horrified.

Julie turned round nervously. 'Oh, hello Mum.' There was an awkward silence. 'Mum, this is Gill. Gill, this is my mum.'

For once Gill was lost for words as he mumbled 'Nice to meet you' in the face of Mrs Warner's frozen stare.

'And do you go to this youth club place as well, er . . . ?' asked Mrs Warner in a voice that had icicles dripping off it.

'Gill,' he said. 'Yeah, sometimes. But the Grove ain't a youth club.'

'Really?' Mrs Warner's eyebrows rose. 'Well, whatever it is I'm not at all sure it's a suitable place for my

51

daughter. Julie, get in the car, please.'

Julie hesitated, not wanting to leave Gill with this horrid atmosphere between them. Wanting to explain that her mum wasn't really like this – that back home in Wimbledon she'd been altogether different.

'Get in the car, Julie,' repeated Mrs Warner in a tone that brooked no nonsense.

Julie gave Gill a final wretched look, but had no choice. As Mrs Warner drove off, Julie took a last look back at where Gill was still standing on the pavement, hoping against hope for an understanding smile. But his pride wouldn't let him show her how much he hated being treated like dirt by that snobby mother of hers. Stuff her. Stuff them all. Shrugging his shoulders as if it was all like water off a duck's back, he turned and walked quickly after Donna, Cas, Winston and Speedy.

CHAPTER THREE

Winston was sitting at a table in the general room, giving Duncan Fergus Robert Mcdonald his orders. Duncan's name was the biggest thing about him. He and Spuggie Campbell shared the same depressing problem – they were both small for their age. 'It's even worse for a *man*,' poor Duncan would moan to Spuggie whenever she'd condescend to listen, but he seldom got any sympathy.

'If anybody asks, you're thirteen, right?' Winston instructed.

'Right,' Duncan chorused obediently.

But Winston hadn't finished yet. 'You gotta be convincing, man,' he warned sternly.

'I will,' promised Duncan. Winston still eyed him doubtfully. 'How old are you anyway?'

'Twelve.' As luck would have it Duncan was two weeks younger than Spuggie, a fact which she seldom let him forget. Every time somebody took something out on Spuggie – which often happened – she took it out on Duncan. From that point of view, he was quite handy. He didn't complain much.

'You look about six,' Winston said. But Duncan was desperate. 'It's for the *Hoppings*, Win!' he implored. In the end Winston graciously agreed to see what he could do. 'Leave it with me. Win'll fix it!' he promised. 'Now bog off, man.'

As Duncan trotted away obediently, and another kid took his place, Winston grinned to himself in gleeful anticipation of all the commission he'd soon be making. With the Hoppings coming up, the rest of the kids would also be dead keen to make as much extra cash as they could.

At the snack bar, Rajeev and Alison were explaining about the Hoppings to Mrs O'Malley. 'It's a ginormous fair on the Town Moor, Mary. Happens every June. It's an old Newcastle tradition,' said Rajeev.

Alison winked. 'Play your cards right and he'll take you on the ghost train,' she promised.

Mrs O'Malley took it all in her stride. 'So long as he doesn't buy me no toffee apples,' she said. 'Not with my dentures.'

While Winston was busy with his transactions, Gill and Speedy were outside on the football pitch kicking a ball around with Ian Webster, a good-looking fifteen-year-old who was seldom seen at the Grove without his little brother and two sisters in tow. Four-year-old Sally, seven-year-old Sammy and nine-year-old Stuart were right little pests, the other kids reckoned, but as Ian was a big lad they mostly kept their complaints to themselves.

'What happened to that bird you fancied, Gill?' Ian asked as he headed the ball in Speedy's direction. 'Posh bit.'

'He means Julie Warner,' said Speedy, neatly intercepting the ball and lofting it over to Gill.

'I know who he means,' Gill commented casually. 'Not seen her,' he added, doing what he liked to think of as his Maradona impression, dribbling the ball neatly down the field.

Even if Gill gave the impression that he couldn't care less, the truth was he'd been coming to the Grove every day hoping Julie would turn up there again. Since that awful night when her cow of a mother had whizzed her away, he'd not seen or heard from her. Maybe he never would. Not that it mattered. She was just another bird. Plenty more where she came from. Still. He did have the hanky she'd given him to wipe the muck off his face after the punch-up with Speedy. He ought to give it back – least he could do. But he didn't even know where she lived. He kicked the ball so hard it cleared the high stone wall at the far end of the pitch and went bouncing into the road.

As Gill was pondering what to do, Julie was walking along the waterfront with Hayley. The two girls, both still in their school uniforms, stood and leaned against the railings, looking at the boats and the lacy network of all the bridges as they arched across the grey expanse of the Tyne.

In a subdued voice, Julie told Hayley how her mum had over-reacted when she'd seen her and Gill together. She wouldn't listen to Julie's protests, she'd managed to convince both herself and Julie's dad that the kids who hung out at Byker Grove were all a bunch of yobbos.

Hayley was upset for her new friend. She knew how lonely she was, and that she'd just begun to enjoy going to the Grove. 'Can't you stand up to them?' she asked.

Julie sighed and looked even more unhappy as she explained that the atmosphere at home was bad enough since they'd moved, and she didn't want to do anything to make it worse.

She smiled gratefully at Hayley. 'It was smashing of you to come. I had to talk to somebody, I've got nobody else.' She hesitated, then asked, 'Would you do me a favour?'

Hayley could guess what it was. 'You want me to speak to Gill.'

Julie took an envelope from her school bag. 'Just give him this.'

Hayley sighed. 'Slap my face if you want, but he's not worth it, Julie.'

Julie just looked at her sadly, as she said, 'I only want to say goodbye.'

Meanwhile in the office at Byker Grove, Geoff was talking to Spuggie and Fraser. A campsite had finally been chosen for the trip. It was to be at a beautiful place called Finchale Priory, on the banks of the River Wear. Most of the kids were wildly enthusiastic, but each time it was mentioned to Fraser and Spuggie they had said they weren't interested. Geoff didn't believe this. He was more certain than ever that there was something seriously wrong.

'It'll be grand fun,' he told them now. 'We'll be doing canoeing, swimming, abseiling, adventure trails in the woods, everything. It's a smashing spot.' He saw the longing in their eyes, and asked gently, 'Is there some sort of problem?' Byker Grove camping trips weren't expensive – Geoff and the other organisers did their best to keep the costs down. And parents who couldn't afford even the small amount involved were allowed to pay it off at so much a week.

Spuggie looked anxiously at her brother, who had flushed a bright angry red. 'Look, there's no blimmin' law says we have to go, is there?' he demanded.

'No. No law at all,' Geoff agreed. And decided to leave the matter there – for the time being.

As soon as they were out of Geoff's earshot, Spuggie said wistfully to Fraser, 'I'd love to go abseiling.' Then she added, 'What's abseiling?'

Fraser answered her fiercely. 'Shut it, Spuggie. Just shut it, eh?' He wished she didn't ask so many questions. He wished things were different. He wished he was eighteen and a full-grown man. He wished he didn't spend so much stupid time wishing for impossible things.

56

In Donna's room, Nicola was sprawled on the frilly pink bedspread painting Shimmering Kandy on her nails as Donna changed out of her school uniform. Being on their own in here was their favourite thing – swapping make-up, gossip and innermost secrets. Nicola wasn't especially envious that Donna had a pretty bedroom like this all to herself, while she had to share a shabby, untidy one with two of her younger sisters. She knew that one day she'd have a room just like it, or maybe better. With a great big bed with heart-shaped satin cushions and a fluffy white rug you could sink into up to your ankles, and a fireplace with a real fire, just like she'd seen on telly. She wasn't sure how she was going to achieve this miracle, but she knew that she would, just as she knew that one day she'd be rich and famous, too.

There was a gentle tap at the door. 'Donna, love, can I come in?' a husky female voice enquired.

Donna pulled a face and called back rudely, 'No, I'm busy.'

That was Lisa, her dad's latest girlfriend, she explained offhandedly. 'She's meant to be a model. She thinks she's gorgeous, but I think she's a big-headed cow.' Privately, Nicola doubted that Lisa was quite as unpleasant as Donna painted her. She was well aware that Donna took a dislike to any of her dad's girlfriends on principle. The principle being that Donna firmly intended to remain the only apple of her doting father's eye, and woe betide any female foolish enough to threaten competition.

Twenty minutes later Nicola was becoming impatient as Donna posed in front of her dressing table mirror, putting yet more gooey gel on her hair. Nicola wanted to get to the Grove. Ian Webster usually came on a Tuesday and she quite fancied him, even if he did always have those pesky little kids tagging along. True, he'd never shown any particular interest in her, but perhaps he needed some encouragement. She was getting fed up with Donna acting like the only one who could get a boyfriend. You'd think she and Cas were practically *engaged* the way she talked.

'I hate my hair,' Donna finally announced. Nicola pulled a face. Donna was *always* going on about her blimmin' hair. 'I think I'll have it cut dead short. Half an inch all over and dye it platinum blonde like Yazz.'

Nicola grinned at the idea. 'You dad'd go bonkers.'

'I can do what I like,' Donna shrugged. 'It's my hair. Same colour as me mum's,' she added casually. 'Least it was last time I saw her.'

It was nearly a year since Mrs Bell had suddenly packed her bags and left the Byker Arms. Nobody quite knew the whole story. Some said it was because she and Jim Bell were always arguing, others that she had gone off with another man. Whatever the truth of it, Donna rarely mentioned her.

'D'you never speak to her now?' Nicola asked carefully. The subject of Donna's mum was a very dodgy area, usually best avoided. But as Donna had mentioned her, Nicola felt it was OK to ask a casual question. She'd always liked Mrs Bell, a slim, pretty woman who wore totally fantastic clothes. She intended to look like Mrs Bell one day. Her own mum was nice enough – in fact she was great. She was always laughing and she'd listen if you had a problem. But she slopped about in tatty old jumpers and skirts and she was still quite fat from her last baby. Nicola eyed her own slender body in the wardrobe mirror. She was *never* going to get fat. If having babies made you fat, then she was never going to have babies either.

'Don't you want to know what she's doing?' Nicola persisted.

'I couldn't care less, I hate her,' Donna finally answered, scowling. Her scowl deepened as Lisa knocked on the door again, saying she really would like a word. Ungraciously, Donna opened the door. Nicola eyed the young woman who entered with undisguised interest.

In her late twenties, Lisa Harris was glamorous in a tarty sort of way, but in spite of her flashy appearance, she had nice eyes and a friendly smile.

'What do you want? We're going out,' Donna said insolently. Lisa finally lost her patience. 'I *was* going to ask you to model at a fashion show, but as you're obviously far too busy . . .' and with that she went out. Donna and Nicola looked at each other.

Nicola was the first to make it to the hallway downstairs, where Lisa was just about to go out with Jim Bell. 'This fashion show, do you mean one with a proper catwalk and that?'

Lisa explained that it was for charity and they were short of a young teenage model. Nicola's eyes widened, as she suddenly saw herself sauntering down the catwalk like a junior Jerry Hall. They'd all be there in the audience, all her school mates and her pals from Byker Grove, and it'd certainly make that Ian Webster sit up and take notice! He'd be so knocked out he'd beg her to go on a date with him. She wouldn't say yes right away, she'd keep him dangling for a bit . . . Then a familiar voice broke into her delicious daydream. 'Go on then, I'll do it, if it's for a good cause,' she heard Donna say. And swallowing a large helping of humble pie she added, 'I'm sorry, Lisa, I didn't mean to be rude. I had a headache.'

As Nicola snorted her disgust at this barefaced lie,

Donna's dad asked if they couldn't both do it, but Lisa said it was mostly women's fashions and they only needed one junior girl. 'But if you two want to toss a coin for it . . .' she added, only to be interrupted by Donna.

Shamelessly she stared Nicola straight in the eye. 'We don't need to toss for it. I'm doing it,' she announced. 'Anyway, she's *my* dad's girlfriend,' and with that she linked her arm chummily through Lisa's as though she was suddenly her best friend in the whole world.

A few streets away, in the corner shop, Mr Patel was eyeing Duncan doubtfully. Winston had sworn that Duncan was thirteen, but he certainly didn't look like a thirteen-year-old to Mr Patel. Winston saw his longed-for commission vanishing before his eyes, and decided that emergency measures were called for. 'He's very small for his age. Runs in the family. Mum. Dad. Brothers. Cousins. All little titches, right, Dunc?' Prompted by a fierce jab in the ribs, Duncan nodded his agreement.

Eventually Mr Patel reluctantly agreed that Duncan could start his paper round the following day. Delighted, Duncan followed Winston out of the shop, already busy planning which ride he'd go on first, when he finally got to the fair. The Divebombers – they were definitely his favourite. On the other hand, the Waltzer was ace. Then there was the Ghost Train, and . . . Oh, heck, it was so exciting he could hardly bear to think about it.

In the kitchen at Byker Grove, Fraser was cautiously showing his new watch to Mrs O'Malley. He'd tried very hard to keep it a secret, but winning something was no fun if you couldn't share it with anyone. He had no special mate among the boys, and he certainly didn't trust any of the girls, they were forever chattering and giggling together in corners. In spite of her sharp tongue, this funny old woman seemed to understand him somehow.

'Aye, it's grand is that. You must be a clever lad.'

'Not really. I was just lucky,' he said modestly. 'Only I'd rather you didn't tell anyone else. You know what they're like. They'd just take the mickey.'

Mrs O'Malley sensed there was more to it than this, but wisely she didn't press him. 'If you don't want me to, then I won't. But thank you for showing it to me. And I still think you're very clever,' she smiled, as she craftily slid an egg sandwich towards him. 'Tell me if I've put enough salt on these,' she said.

'Hey, Cas, guess what!' Donna called out loudly as she came into the general room, 'I'm going to be a model!' Nicola was definitely feeling cheesed off with her friend by now, and Donna only made matters worse by batting her eyelashes at Ian, who wanted to be a professional photographer one day. 'You can take the photos for my portfolio, Ian, when I'm a top model,' she crowed, and added, for Nicola's benefit, 'that's what models have – all their pictures in a portfolio. Lisa told me.' She tossed her hair in what she obviously thought was a sexy, model-girl fashion and went off to the snack bar with Cas, slinking her hips.

Nicola was pleased to see that Ian wasn't much impressed by Donna's airs and graces. Instead he was staring at Nicola with a thoughtful expression. 'You'd be good,' he said.

'Oh yes? What as?' Nicola asked suspiciously. If he was going to come out with some clever crack, he'd find her more than his match.

'A photographic subject.' He wasn't sending her up, he was quite serious. 'You've got good bones.'

Nicola giggled. 'First time anybody's complimented me on me bones,' she said. But she liked the way he was looking at her. She liked it even better when he asked, 'Can I take your picture some time?'

She was wondering whether to say yes there and then, or keep him waiting, when little Stuart, never far away, tugged at Ian's sleeve.

'Yes?' Ian said impatiently.

'She feels sick,' whispered Stuart, as Sammy hung her head.

Ian sighed. Just the sort of thing you needed when you were chatting up a girl. But Nicola was OK about it, she didn't take the mickey like some of the others would have done. 'Don't you ever get brassed off having to cart them everywhere?' she asked sympathetically.

'Stupid question,' said Ian rather rudely. But she understood. It was his situation he was angry with, not her.

'So why do you do it?' It seemed as if she genuinely wanted to know. He shrugged. 'Haven't much choice, have I? My mum's a one-parent family. She works night shift. Ain't easy for her neither.'

Nicola found herself offering to take Sammy to the girls' loo. She firmly believed in equality. *If* she ever did get married and have kids, her husband would share the chores fifty-fifty, no danger. But still, a big lad like that being permanently lumbered. It didn't seem right.

As she led Sammy out, an excited Winston hurtled through the door. 'Hey, Gill. Speedy. Cas. Anybody else who wants to make a few bob, I've got one well cool caper lined up!'

There was a general buzz of interest at this, especially from Spuggie. 'Me, me. I'll do it!' she yelled, bouncing

62

up and down in her eagerness. She was highly miffed when Winston said, 'Sorry, you're out.'

'Why? That's not fair!' Her pique only increased when he explained, 'It's men only. Heavy work, piles of stuff to be shifted. Needs muscle, that!'

'Huh!' jeered Spuggie. 'You mean little skinny marbles like yours?'

But Winston wasn't fazed. 'I'm the organiser, Shortstuff.' He tapped his head significantly, indicating his super-abundance of brains. Spuggie could only watch indignantly as Winston gathered a group of lads about him, and gave them the plan for the following day. They were all to meet at four o'clock sharp, straight from school, and Winston would lead them to The Job. Duncan let out a yell of anguish as Spuggie kicked him on the shins. 'What's that for?' But Spuggie didn't bother to answer. She just had to kick something, and he happened to be nearby. Why was she *never* allowed to do anything? It wasn't fair.

As Winston finished giving the lads their instructions, Hayley came over and asked Gill if she could have a word. Aware that she usually had no time for him, he followed curiously as she led him into a quiet corner of the hall outside.

'She asked me to give you this,' Hayley said, taking a pink envelope out of her pocket. He didn't need to ask who. As he ripped open the envelope, Hayley couldn't help herself. 'I told her she was daft,' she said. But he was too busy reading the note that Julie had written.

The next afternoon Winston was waiting at the meeting place, by the wooden tower in the adventure playground. So far only Cas had turned up. Winston tapped his foot impatiently. What was the point of *organising* them if they didn't blimmin' turn up to be organised?

There was he, burning up all his precious brain power to get them some blimmin' *cash*, and they couldn't even be bothered to show up on time! Finally Speedy rode up on his bike. 'About time too, man,' said Winston crossly. When he was boss of his own multinational corporation, they'd all better turn up on time or *else*!

Winston brightened as Gill showed up next, closely followed by Ian. Then he saw Sammy, Sally and Stuart tagging along behind Ian. 'They're not coming,' he stated flatly.

'In that case, I don't come,' retorted Ian.

Winston sighed. Why was everybody so blimmin' *difficult*? And he was doing them the favour! There was no gratitude. He looked warily up at Ian, who towered above his head, and sighed. 'All right. They can come. But they're not to touch nothing, mind.' He glared at Sally, Sammy and Stuart, who promptly stuck their tongues out at him. 'Right, let's get this show on the road,' he ordered.

But now it was Gill's turn to put a spanner in the works. 'You'll have to count me out,' he said.

Winston fixed him with an indignant look. Surely you were entitled to expect your best mate to support your efforts? But it was no use, Gill was no longer interested. 'I thought you said you wanted a piece of the action, man?' Winston pleaded.

'Yeah, well, gotta go somewhere, haven't I?' said Gill, looking oddly embarrassed.

'Bet it's something to do with that stupid London bird,' Winston muttered to himself, as he led his little army off before it dwindled any further.

As soon as they had disappeared round the corner, Gill took the by now crumpled pink note from his pocket and read it for the umpteenth time.

'Please meet me at the Monument, four o'clock. Julie.'

As he read it, he wondered why he'd bothered. He needed more aggro from that snooty bird and her snooty mother like a hole in the head. Why didn't he just catch up with the others and earn himself some cash? Brush 'ead seemed to think there was good money to be made from whatever it was he'd got lined up. And he could definitely use some extra dosh.

At the Monument, Julie was nervously scanning people's faces as they walked past. She wasn't sure if he'd come – and if he did come, what sort of mood he'd be in. But she knew she had to try and set the record straight. Suddenly her face lit up, as she waved. 'Hey, Gill! Over here!' Thank goodness.

'I just wanted to explain. Why I didn't come back to the Grove. I thought you might be wondering,' she added lamely.

His eyes were still cold and unfriendly as he answered, 'Your business, girl.'

She stood uncertainly, not knowing what to say to him next. Still unsmiling, he suggested they go for a coffee.

At the café they found a table and Julie tried to explain. 'I'm sorry my mum was so horrible to you. She's all right, really. It's just moving here, that's what she hates. And with me being an only child, they've always been a bit protective. You know what they're like.'

Gill was deliberately tough. 'No, I don't,' he said, tipping some sugar from the bowl onto the table in little heaps.

'You've got parents.'

'Not like them. Couldn't care less what I do,' he said.

Julie wasn't sure that she found this an appealing prospect. 'Don't you mind?' she asked hesitantly.

'Tell you what I would mind, girl. Being treated like a little pet dog. Do this, do that.' He drew patterns with the sugar on the plastic table top.

She tried to tell him it wasn't like that, but he didn't seem to want to even try and understand. 'Nothing to stop you walking out,' he said.

'I'm fourteen years old, Gill!' Surely he couldn't be serious?

'Not permanent, cloth-head.' There was the first glimmer of a smile in his dark eyes. 'You want to go to the Grove, you go. What can they do?' But she knew she couldn't defy them. She wasn't made like that.

'Will I see you?' He scooped the sugar back into the bowl. The man behind the counter frowned, but was too busy serving customers to come over and tell him off.

'I don't think so,' she sighed. 'I just wanted to see you today to explain.'

'Right, then. You've explained. Better trot along home now, hadn't you, like a good little girl. You want to be a doormat, Yorkie, down to you. But nobody treads on Gill. Not now, not ever.'

Julie was close to tears as she stood up and ran out of the snack bar. It was stupid to have expected him to understand. Nicola and Donna were right. He was nothing but a big loud-mouthed yobbo. What had she ever seen in him, anyway?

As she walked along, she felt a sudden tap on her shoulder. Gill was holding out a now clean but crumpled hanky. 'I've washed it. Most of the blood's come out.'

'Thank you. You needn't have bothered, it was only

66

an old one.' She knew that didn't sound very friendly, but she wasn't sure what else to say. Besides, *he* hadn't been very friendly.

'Right, then.' He turned to go. She watched him walk a few yards.

'Gill.' She didn't know why she'd stopped him. It would be best just to let him walk out of her life. At least that way she wouldn't get any more aggro at home. She shut her mind to the memory of what it was like at home these days. The silences were worse than the arguments, with Mum looking so sad all the time and Dad sleeping in the spare room. And the worst thing was, she felt somehow it was all her fault.

Gill was standing looking at her, waiting for her to speak. She took a deep breath. 'Why did you take that motorbike? Weren't you scared of getting caught?' she asked.

He looked her straight in the eye as he answered, 'That's what it's all about, taking risks. Got to stick your neck out some time, duchess.'

Julie got the message. 'You think I'm pathetic, don't you?' she demanded.

'Yeah.' Well, what else did she expect him to say? She was shaken for a moment. He really could be a swine when he wanted. But she had asked him. And he was only telling her the truth.

'I'll speak to them,' she resolved. 'I'm not some little toy they own. I'm practically a woman. I've got my rights.' Even as she spoke, she knew she meant it. If he made another of his sarcastic cracks, heaven help her, she'd slap his arrogant face. But he was smiling at her, with the cheeky, friendly grin that had so attracted her that first evening she'd gone to Byker Grove. 'Attagirl.' He gave her a huge wink. 'Go for it, Yorkie.'

And Julie knew she was going to make one final effort

to change her mum's mind, no matter what the consequences.

Meanwhile Winston was leading his little procession along the street, with Sammy, Sally, Stuart and Popeye trotting behind. Finally they came to a halt in front of a large but run-down old house with a garage built onto the side. Winston led them up the path and with some difficulty thrust open the rickety garage door. 'This is it!' he said proudly, as if ushering them into the *Starship Enterprise*. There was a gasp of disbelief.

Old newspapers, empty bottles, carpets, broken furniture, cans of paint, even a rusty pram – the garage was piled to the ceiling with junk! Five pairs of eyes turned accusingly on Winston. Even Popeye looked worried.

'Yeah, well, I did say there was a fair bit of graft involved . . .' he began.

'Fair bit of graft?' Ian, like the rest of them, was totally staggered. 'Clearing this lot out? Be quicker to knock it down and build a new one.'

'Oh, well, if you want to bottle out,' Winston began casually, but realising they might well take him up on it, he quickly did a deal, and offered to cut his commission if they'd get stuck in. 'After all,' he wheedled, 'you're here now. Be daft to come all this way for nothing.' Reluctantly, Cas, Speedy and Ian rolled up their sleeves and trooped inside.

They'd all been working hard for some time when suddenly Ian noticed that Sally, Sammy and Stuart had disappeared. He and Cas looked round and saw Popeye sniffing round a pile of cardboard boxes which they had stacked neatly ready for the salvage department to collect. Right on top of the pyramid was a large empty carton which had once contained a washing machine.

At least, it had been empty when the boys had heaved it up there, but now it was wriggling about in a most peculiar fashion. Strange little giggling sounds came from inside.

'Sammy? Sally? Stu? You in there?' Ian called. But before he could investigate further, Popeye, delighted to have beaten him to it, jumped up to join his new chums, and the whole lot came tumbling down, in a welter of broken bits of cardboard, polystyrene chippings and flying arms and legs.

Winston was just about to make some scathing remark when he saw the look on Ian's face, and thought better of it. 'OK, let's call it a day,' he announced wearily, hoping that tomorrow some miracle might happen – like a flying saucer spiriting those pesky little kids off to another galaxy millions of light years away. It was more than a man could stand.

The rest of them wearily made their way back to the Grove, but Winston's work wasn't finished yet. Staggering under the weight of a carton of empty pop bottles he called in to see Mr Patel. 'How much'll you give us for this lot, Mr Patel? And there's more where these came from,' he asked hopefully. Money on the empties was down to him. Boss's perks.

But Mr Patel glared at him furiously and pointed to the door. 'Out!'

'No need to be like that, Mr P. They're not nicked.' But it wasn't the empties that were upsetting Mr Patel. Winston now noticed Duncan standing miserably by the door, as Mr Patel fixed him with a steely look. 'Thirteen, you said!'

Winston in turn glared at Rajeev, who had appeared from the back of the shop. 'You flippin' grassed,' he accused.

But Duncan wretchedly explained that the

authorities had come round checking up on all the paper lads and girls.

'You tell me he has a permit!' raged Mr Patel.

'Er, I said it was in the pipeline, like. He'll get it on his birthday.' Winston diplomatically omitted to mention that was six months away. But it didn't make any difference.

'Out,' repeated Mr Patel firmly, pointing once again at the door.

Winston knew his rights. 'What about his wages?' he asked.

'It's all right, he's give me some money,' said Duncan.

'He's lucky I do. I am a respectable shopkeeper. You get me in serious trouble, boy,' said Mr P, beginning to dance about with rage again.

Winston decided it was better to leave before Mr Patel could shriek 'Out' at him again. He was beginning to get a headache.

On the way back to the Grove, Winston asked Duncan for his commission.

'What commission? You said you'd get me a job. Some job. I only worked a blimmin' day!' Duncan was almost as indignant as Mr Patel had been. Winston sighed. You tried to do people a favour and all you got was a load of earache. What with those pesky kids at the garage, and now Duncan, he wondered why he bothered.

He hadn't noticed Rajeev walking along behind them. 'I think we forget the commission, don't you, Winston?' he said quietly. He was not only much older than Winston, he was also a couple of feet taller and he had pretty powerful shoulders on him. 'Well, yeah. In the circumstances, I'll let you off, man,' said Winston magnanimously, and fled into the Grove.

In the general room, the girls were having an informal dance session, bopping energetically to the latest Michael Jackson LP. But Donna was getting up everyone's nose. Because she was going to be in a fashion show, she seemed to think that automatically made her the Byker Grove disco queen.

She was showing off so much that Nicola started to say, 'Just 'cos you think you're the second Jasmin le flippin' Bon Bon doesn't mean you're totally brilliant at everything . . .' when she broke off as her eyes were drawn towards the door.

All the other girls in the room, including Alison, watched fascinated as Geoff entered with a knockout-looking young man. In white T-shirt, designer jeans and beautifully cut leather jacket, he looked, Donna and Nicola agreed later, like a cross between Tom Cruise and Rob Lowe. With a dash of George Michael thrown in. But it wasn't just the younger girls who responded instantly to the stranger's charisma. Passing the snack bar he winked cheerfully at Mrs O'Malley, saying, 'Well, well, if it isn't Miss Ellie!' And when he bought and ate a slice of her home-made slab cake, he gained a devoted slave for life.

Donna, as usual, was the first to speak up. 'Hi, I'm Donna, who are you?' she asked, all big eyes and dimples.

'Steve Bradley. Call me Brad,' he smiled.

Geoff explained that Brad was going to show them how to do basic photography, starting the following week.

'Hey, yeah, I was going to sign up for that,' Donna said without blinking. Nicola couldn't let her get away with that. 'You never were, lying cow!'

Then Geoff introduced Brad to Alison, and Nicola and Donna promptly forgot their feud. They dug each other knowingly in the ribs when they saw how she looked at him. 'Like, wow, man!' they agreed later.

The next day, Speedy and Winston were messing around in the adventure playground, while Spuggie and Popeye chased each other in hectic circles, when Cas rolled up on a brand-new skateboard. His mum and dad had given it to him for his birthday.

'Brilliant! Can I have a go?' asked Spuggie eagerly.

'No.' Cas wasn't being unkind, but he'd only just got it. He didn't want it getting smashed up before he'd even had a chance to try it out.

Just then a beaten-up but snazzy little sports car drove up, and Brad vaulted out onto the pavement. 'Hi, guys.' He looked at the skateboard with interest. 'That's a real beaut. Whose is it?'

'Cas's. It's his birthday,' said Spuggie importantly. She always liked to be first with the news.

'Mind if I try it?'

'He won't let you,' Spuggie said. But she was wrong.

'Sure,' Cas answered, ignoring Spuggie's indignant 'Huh!' This Brad looked like the kind of guy who could do anything.

He was right. They all watched open-mouthed as Brad went into a dazzling routine, swooping at speed up and down the wooden ramps in the playground, and finishing by leaping expertly over the litterbin and coming to a neat halt in front of them.

Even Gill, who had just arrived on the scene, was impressed.

'Where did you learn to do that?' asked Spuggie, gazing up at Brad in awe.

He explained that he'd got hooked on skateboarding when he was just a little kid, about the same age as young Stuart. He'd even had some crazy idea of turning pro, until he'd switched his attention to cameras.

'Could you teach me?' begged Spuggie.

'You're too small, titch,' Gill responded automatically.

'She's not, actually,' said Brad. 'She'd be great.'

'See, blimmin' know-all,' said Spuggie triumphantly, and she practically floated back into the Grove with the rest of them.

Brad came into the general room looking like the Pied Piper of Hamelin, with Gill, Cas, Winston, Speedy, Spuggie and Duncan hot on his heels. As he studied the noticeboard to check how many people had signed up for photography, Geoff went up to Fraser, who was sitting as usual with his head buried in a book. 'Are you not doing the photography, Fraser? I don't see your name down,' he asked.

When Fraser gruffly replied that he wasn't interested, Geoff was surprised. 'No? I'd have thought you would be, you're so good at anything technical. Look at the way you won that watch . . .'

Fraser looked up at that, his face scarlet, but it was too late. Spuggie's sharp little ears missed nothing, and she leapt in with 'What watch? You never said you won a watch, Fraser!' As Spuggie's shrill voice penetrated every corner of the room, Fraser looked more furious than ever.

Geoff realised too late that he had put his foot right in it. 'I'm sorry, lad,' he said. 'I forgot it was secret.' But this didn't make things any better. 'What watch?' demanded Spuggie insistently. 'What flippin' watch? Why was it secret?'

This was the last straw for the normally quiet boy. Shut up, will you, Spuggie?' He glared furiously at Geoff. 'You did that on purpose, didn't you? Had to go and blow it! I shouldn't have flaming trusted you! I'll never trust you again!' And with that he stormed out, leaving a shocked and silenced room.

Geoff went after him, and caught him by the shoulder just as he was going through the front door. 'All right, lad,' he said quietly. 'Do you want to tell me what's really bothering you? I can't help if I don't know what's wrong.'

But Fraser insisted there was nothing wrong. 'Just keep your nose out, that's all. Keep your blimmin' nose out!' he said, wiping back angry tears, as he left. Geoff had no choice but to let him go.

In the kitchen, Rajeev was lifting a teapot down off a high shelf for Mrs O'Malley when she looked at him worriedly. 'Can't he do something?' she asked.

'Who?' Rajeev put the teapot down on the table.

'Him, Geoffrey. There's something definitely not right with them two, poor little mites.'

Rajeev explained to her that Geoff was in a tricky situation. He had no authority to go barging into the kids' home lives. If he thought there was something wrong, all he could do was tip off the social services. After that it was their responsibility.

This didn't satisfy Mrs O'Malley. 'Take forever, with all that red tape,' she sniffed. Then she looked at Rajeev with a sly gleam in her eye. 'They don't pay you for coming here, do they, lad?' she asked.

'Heck, no,' Rajeev smiled. 'I'm just a part-time volunteer.'

'So, if you're not official,' she said craftily, 'there'd be no red tape to stop *you* having a little sniff around, would there?'

In the Warners' living room, Julie's mum and dad were sitting in tense silence when Julie walked in.

'Mum. Dad. I want to talk to you,' she said. They

74

both looked up, aware of a new note of determination in her voice.

'It's about the Grove . . .' she began, but her mother interrupted her. 'Julie,' she said sadly, as she put her sewing down. 'We've been through all that.'

But Julie wasn't to be put off. In a firm voice she told them that she did understand that they wanted to protect her from what they thought of as bad influences. 'But the kids who go there aren't bad. In fact they're great, most of them. You'd realise that if you gave yourselves a chance to get to know them. I don't want to upset you again, Mum, but I'm not a little girl any more, I'm nearly fifteen. And I've made my mind up. I'm going back to Byker Grove. Whatever you say.'

CHAPTER FOUR

The train pulled up at the Metro Station and Gill jumped out eagerly. 'Come on, Brush 'ead!' he called to Winston as he raced along into the Metro Centre. Winston slouched sulkily behind. He hated rushing on a Saturday morning. Rest of the week was bad enough, when he had to go to blimmin' school. Saturdays were for getting up late and eating bacon butties and watching telly and just messing about. Forget this crack of dawn stuff, man – today it was only just gone nine and Gill had already dragged him here. Besides, they were supposed to be going to this Walker Wheels place later with Brad. If they hung around the Metro Centre too long they'd miss it.

They were running up the down escalators when the light dawned. Winston saw that Gill had suddenly turned and was running back down the escalator after a girl with short dark hair. 'Hey, Yorkie!' he called, but as the girl turned round he saw she was a stranger. 'So that's it,' Winston muttered disgustedly to himself. 'So that's why we got here before the place was blimmin' open!'

Gill sighed. He had enough on his plate without Winston giving him hassle. He wondered whether Julie would have the guts to confront that snobby mother of hers. And if he'd ever see her again. He was probably wasting his time here. Even if she did come to the Metro Centre on a Saturday morning shopping trip, with his luck he'd bump into her in one of the cafés, smiling that slow, shy, dark-eyed smile at some big prat from her school. Like the ones he'd seen around with their fancy green blazers. He kicked a harmless litterbin ferociously at the thought.

In the Warners' living room, Julie's mum was vacuuming when her husband walked in. 'Right, I'm off to golf,' he said cheerfully, kissing her on the cheek. There was no reaction from his wife.

'What's the matter?' he asked.

'We talked about going shopping,' she replied, her mouth set in a thin, unhappy line.

'Fine. We'll do that, then.' He was willing to do anything which might improve the awful atmosphere between them these days. But Mrs Warner didn't respond. 'No, you go to golf, I've things to do around the house,' she told him. He sighed. He felt as if he just couldn't win. 'Clare, this is ridiculous,' he began, but just then Julie walked into the room. She'd obviously spent a lot of time on her appearance, her dark hair had been brushed till it shone, and the pink jacket she was wearing cast a rosy glow on her clear skin.

'Right, I'll be home in time for supper,' she said, a little too brightly. There was a silence. Ever since Julie had told them that whatever they said, she was going back to Byker Grove, the subject had hung in the air like an unanswered question. Now Julie was clearly showing them that she meant to back her words with actions. If there was going to be a showdown, this was it.

Mr Warner felt that his wife was being too hard on Julie, banning her from the Grove. Ever since that night, they'd had the same argument over and over again. Mr Warner would say his wife was over-reacting and making a mountain out of a molehill. Mrs Warner would reply that *he* hadn't seen Julie tenderly kissing the bloodstained face of some young hoodlum who had obviously been in a fight. 'These just aren't the sort of young people I want my daughter to mix with, Michael,' Mrs Warner had said angrily. 'I know she needs to make friends up here, but taking up with a bunch of yobbish louts is not what I had in mind!'

'She's not made any friends at school yet, and if she has taken to some of the kids at Byker Grove I don't see any real harm in letting her go there,' he'd replied. 'Julie's not a child any more, I think we have to learn to trust her judgement. And if she does make some mistakes along the way, well, that's all part and parcel of growing up.'

'Even if she gets hurt?'

'That's part of growing up too. We can't wrap her up in cotton wool, Clare.'

Now both he and Julie waited tensely, as Mrs Warner looked at her daughter. 'Just watch who you mix with, love,' she said finally. Julie realised that this was as close to consent as she'd get. She kissed her mother gratefully. 'I'll be fine,' she said. And then she added 'Mum, Dad . . . thanks,' before she turned and ran happily out of the room.

Michael and Clare Warner exchanged unhappy glances. They both knew it wasn't just the thought of Julie going back to Byker Grove that was troubling them. The situation between them was rapidly getting out of control. 'This isn't fair to her, keeping her in the dark,' Mrs Warner sighed.

He understood how she felt, as he answered wretchedly, 'But we're pretty much in the dark ourselves right now, aren't we, Clare?'

As Julie walked down the garden path she knew that her problems weren't over yet. Still, for the moment anyway, she could go back to the Grove. It was funny, really. When her dad had first suggested it, she hadn't wanted to go anywhere near the place. Now she couldn't wait to get there. And she didn't really know why. Did she like Byker Grove that much? Or did she just want to get away from the horrible atmosphere at home, where nothing was like it used to be? She could remember a time not so long ago when the three of them were happy, and her mum used to laugh a lot. She hardly ever laughed now.

Cas was waiting for the other lads to show up at the adventure playground outside the Grove. They were all going to Walker Wheels with Brad, and he'd get a chance to learn how to do amazing things on his new skateboard. Cas was looking forward to it, not just for the excitement but because for once it would be great to do something without the girls tagging along. It wasn't that Cas didn't like girls, far from it. But he was beginning to get very cheesed off with the way Donna Bell seemed to treat him as her personal property. She already had her initials on her duffle bag and her Walkman and that gold locket thing she always wore round her neck. Next she'd blimmin' well have D.B. stamped all over him as well.

Fortunately, Donna was unaware of Cas's feelings as she primped happily in front of her bedroom mirror.

'Haven't you finished tarting yourself up yet?' Nicola demanded impatiently. 'If you bung any more of that stuff on, your hair'll rot!'

Donna strutted out of the bedroom, dragging her jacket behind her. 'All the best models use gel, darling. Lisa wears tons.'

'She your flavour of the month now? You couldn't stick her last week,' Nicola said crossly, as she followed Donna down the stairs.

'No way.' Donna was perfectly serious. 'Just a useful business contact for when I'm famous. Donna Bell, Face of the Nineties.'

'Give us a break, Bell,' Nicola snorted scornfully, but Donna was enjoying her fantasy too much.

'Course I'll need a modelling name. Tricia La Belle, Stacey Margarita, Natasha . . .'

'Fifi Lamour, Mandy Mascara . . .'

'Victoria Valentine . . .' By now even Donna could see the funny side, and both girls collapsed on the bottom stair in a fit of giggles.

At the Grove, Cas had now been joined by Speedy, Gill and Winston. Winston had finally managed to convince Gill that looking for the Warner girl was like looking for a needle in a haystack. He'd told him that he'd never find her in that crowd at the Metro Centre even if she was there. 'Which she probably isn't, man,' he couldn't resist adding. 'She's probably gone out somewhere posh with mummy and daddy for the day.'

Then his face dropped as he saw Julie walk up the drive. 'Oh, piggin' hell,' he muttered to himself. He'd really hoped they'd seen the last of her. Gill struggled to stay cool. 'Glad to see you know good advice when it pokes you in the eye, duchess,' he commented, trying not to let her see how pleased he was.

'I decided to stand up for myself,, if that's what you mean,' Julie answered. She wasn't going to tell him how hard it had been.

There was a sudden shout of excitement as Brad finally rolled up, driving a van hired specially for the occasion. 'Why've you come in that?' Naturally it was Speedy who wanted to know. 'Because I'd be hard pushed to fit you lot, a pile of skateboards, and the motorbike in the back of my MG, Speedy,' Brad smiled. The motorbike was one that Winston had 'won' from the garage clearout; they were taking it along to see if they could get it fixed.

In the general room, Donna was swanking to Hayley about what a wonderful life models have. 'Earn hundreds a day, they do. Thousands. And you get whisked off to the Bahamas with gorgeous hunks falling at your feet,' she added.

Hayley wasn't impressed. 'Yeah. And you get to do swimwear in December and fur coats in July.'

Donna frowned. 'What's up with you? You've been dead nowty since you got here. Anyway, it's Saturday. Aren't you supposed to be at work?'

Hayley told her she'd packed it in, because she had too much homework. Donna was too wrapped up in her own forthcoming triumph to give it much thought, or she might have been more curious. They'd all known how pleased Hayley was when she'd got the job. Brad came in to see if anyone else was coming on the Walker Wheels jaunt, and Donna's eyes lit up as she told him she was modelling that afternoon in a proper fashion show.

'She's trying to get you to come,' Nicola chipped in.

'I am not!' said Donna haughtily, then spoilt the effect by adding eagerly, 'Will you?'

She gave Nicola a triumphant look as Brad replied thoughtfully, 'Know what, sweetheart? I might just do that.'

Outside the lads were waiting with increasing impatience, and soon started a chorus of 'Why are we waiting?' Brad came out of the Grove and said, 'Right, we're on our way.'

Just at that moment Spuggie came running up. 'Wait for me, Brad. Wait for me!' she called.

'Oh, heck!' Winston looked disgusted. 'We're not taking blimmin' *girls*, are we?'

'We're taking anyone who wants to come,' Brad said sternly. 'And there's just one Spuggie-sized space left.'

Winston groaned, and Spuggie gave him a cheeky thumbs-up sign as she jumped into the van after the others. But as he moved to board it himself, Winston saw that Gill was still talking to Julie. 'You ready, Gill?' he called.

Gill was torn between his mates and his girl. He'd really wanted to go with the gang, but now Julie had shown up and suddenly Walker Wheels didn't seem so important after all.

As Brad jumped in and started the engine he called out, 'Your mate not coming then, Winston?'

'Nah,' Winston muttered. 'If he wants to stick around with blimmin' birds, he can suit himself.'

When Julie and Gill walked into the general room a few minutes later they found all eyes were on them. Hayley was delighted to see Julie back. 'Hey, you did it!' she grinned.

'We thought you weren't coming back,' said Nicola.

'Yeah, what a nice surprise,' commented Donna coldly. But Julie didn't take any notice of Donna's sarcasm, she was just glad to be here, and even happier that Gill was so obviously pleased to see her again.

Gill wasn't the only one who was delighted that Julie was back at the Grove. 'Julie, can I have a word?' Hayley asked. 'Somewhere private.'

Explaining to a somewhat miffed-looking Gill that she wouldn't be long, Julie followed Hayley up a narrow, twisting flight of stairs and through a skylight onto a small area of the roof which was flat. Strictly speaking it was out of bounds, but just now Hayley needed somewhere where she was sure there wouldn't be any listening ears. Besides, she loved it up here, high above the city with a panoramic view right over Newcastle to the green hills and valleys beyond.

In a low voice, Hayley told Julie that she'd walked out

of her job. 'They accused me of stealing,' she said. Then, as she saw the shocked look on Julie's face, added, 'Well, as good as.' She explained that a woman who was staying at the hotel had lost a valuable ring.

'But why should they say it was you?' Julie demanded indignantly.

'Why d'you think? Because I'm the youngest and the newest and because of this,' she said bitterly, touching her face. Julie looked puzzled. 'Because I'm black, why else? The manager asked me questions like I was already guilty, and the other girls think I am too, I can tell by the way they look at me. I've probably made it worse now by not going back, but I wasn't sticking around the place with them all thinking I was a thief,' she finished.

'That's horrible,' Julie hugged her sympathetically. 'You're better off out of a place like that.'

But Hayley told her they needed the money, and the worst thing was, she hadn't had the courage to tell her mum yet. 'She's got enough to worry about, I don't want to give her any more aggro.' She looked at Julie urgently as they heard footsteps coming up to the roof. 'Promise you won't tell anyone, Julie? Swear?'

Julie gave her friend her solemn oath, as Gill stuck his head impatiently round the skylight. 'You finished nattering yet?' he demanded. Julie was reluctant to leave Hayley, but the other girl said she'd be fine. 'Come on then,' Gill urged, climbing back down the stairs.

'Where to?' Julie wanted to know, following him nevertheless.

But Gill shook his head. 'Gillespie's Tour of New-castle,' was all he'd tell her.

'I've seen a lot of it already,' she laughed.

'Not the sort of places I'm going to take you to, you

haven't,' he winked, as he took her by the hand and led her out of the Grove.

Someone else who was exploring an unfamiliar area of the city was Rajeev. Mary O'Malley hadn't forgotten their last conversation, when she'd slyly suggested to him that he might pay a visit to Fraser and Spuggie's home. She was determined to find out what was making Fraser in particular so very unhappy, and why neither of the Campbell kids was going on the camping trip though both of them were clearly longing to join in. Rajeev knew Geoff wouldn't approve of him sticking his nose in where it didn't belong, but Mary could be very persuasive. And he did want to help Fraser and Spuggie if he could. Now, after several more prods from Mary, he found himself in a grey canyon surrounded by tall tower blocks of council flats. Consulting an address he'd found in the filing cabinet while Geoff was out of the office, he approached one of the blocks. Resolutely, he knocked on the door, but it was already ajar, and swung open at his touch.

'Mr Campbell? Mrs Campbell? Anyone there?' he called nervously, half wishing he hadn't come. What on earth was he going to say? What if they asked him for some credentials? They'd be perfectly entitled to. What would he tell them? That he was just a part-time helper whose only authority was the say-so of an interfering old woman?

There was still no sound from the flat. Tentatively, he pushed the door open wider and stepped straight into the living room. He saw a man, obviously Fraser and Spuggie's dad, apparently fast asleep in a battered old armchair. The room itself was in chaos. It looked as though it hadn't been tidied for a month, and there were empty beer cans everywhere.

'Mr Campbell?' No answer.

Rajeev tried again.

The man stirred. His eyes opened and he looked at Rajeev blankly. His head swayed slightly, he opened his mouth to speak, but no words came out as he fell back into a drunken stupor.

Rajeev turned and walked back out of the door.

Meanwhile Spuggie was briefly able to forget her unhappiness about missing the camping trip. She was too busy having a wonderful time at Walker Wheels, which was a large open site on the river bank in the Walker district of Newcastle. Disturbed by the growing number of kids who nicked bikes and cars for so-called joyriding, the Inner City Partnership had decided to offer them something that was not only legal and safe, but much more fun. Fourteen acres of wasteland had been turned into a paradise for anything on wheels – hence the name. Here, kids raced about on everything from roller skates to skateboards to motorbikes of all kinds. Banks of old tyres marked out a tarmac area where bikes could race round, there was a steeply curved roller slide for skateboards, and there were stomach-churning BMX ramps. Eleven of the fourteen acres of land were rough ground which was made up of different tracks – one of them was a huge bowl which the lads had named 'Death Valley'. Another track on the hillside, again marked out with tyres, was known as the 'Aintree'. Others included 'Claggy Trousers', which was a muddy trench into which most of the bikers fell with a resounding splat at one time or another, and 'Snap Legs', which was a tricky obstacle course including a sharp bend. Kids could either use the project's bikes or bring their own.

Naturally Spuggie had expected the worst when they arrived. 'Bet they don't have any bikes my size,' she muttered glumly to Brad as they all jumped out of the van. 'They never have anything my size.' But Brad just grinned and pointed at a whole line of small bikes parked by the shed, and now, crash-helmeted and mud-spattered, she was happily whizzing round the track, flying over the humps and splashing through the water with the rest of them.

Brad was talking to Mike, one of the resident mechanics at Walker Wheels. He was there to help kids learn how to maintain their bikes, and how to fix them up when they broke down. He looked over the bike Winston and the gang had found at the garage, and said he could get them some cheap second-hand parts.

'Brilliant!' said Cas and Speedy.

'Bet I could get 'em cheaper,' muttered Winston, who was still narked that Gill had let him down in order to go off with Julie Warner.

But Winston was the last person on Gill's mind, as he and Julie walked happily hand in hand along the waterfront. This was just the start of his 'tour'. He knew that Newcastle – 'his' Newcastle –was a colourful and fascinating city, and today he was going to show Julie that she wasn't missing anything by leaving Wimbledon and those smoothy southern lads behind. Today he was going to show her a real man's city.

Donna arrived at the church hall in time to see Lisa finish pinning a pleated drop round the edge of the dais down which the models would walk. 'Ouch,' she said, as a pin stuck in her finger. Jim Bell, who was up on a stepladder fixing the lights, asked anxiously if she was all right. 'I need you to kiss it better,' said Lisa flirtatiously.

Unseen by either of them, Donna felt her heart sink. She hated the way her dad and Lisa seemed to be getting more and more of a cosy couple all the time. Only that morning she'd seen her dad sneaking Lisa out of the Byker Arms early, before they thought Donna would be awake. 'Pathetic,' Donna had said to Nicola later. 'I don't know why he bothers pretending. As if I don't know what goes on. I couldn't really care less if she stays.' That wasn't true, but she wasn't going to admit it to anybody, not even to her best friend.

And she wasn't going to let anything spoil her big day either. She pushed the hurtful thoughts about her dad and Lisa out of her mind, and concentrated on her moment of triumph, when she'd walk down that catwalk and everybody would gasp with astonishment. 'I always knew that Donna Bell was a good-looking girl,' they'd say, 'but I never realised she was sensational.' There might be somebody important in the audience, you never knew. Maybe a top agent, or even a talent scout for TV or films . . . Brooke Shields had started her career as a model at about the same age as Donna, hadn't she? And so had Jodie Foster. Earlier, at the Grove, Alison had warned her not to get too carried away. 'I know this is exciting, but fame and fortune are a long way off yet. I don't want you to be disappointed, pet,' she'd said, and Donna had replied airily that she wasn't expecting anything much, that it was just a lark. But now when Lisa told her she'd collected the dress Donna was to model, and it was a real knockout, Donna felt her heart give a little hop, skip and jump of sheer excitement.

It felt even better when, a short time later, she was seated in the dressing room backstage with the other models. 'Backstage' – the phrase had a magical ring to it. As she carefully added another coat of mascara to her already overloaded eyelashes, she glanced sidelong at the pretty girl sitting next to her. Belinda was about twenty, and she was applying blusher with practised ease. 'Course this isn't my first time,' Donna found herself saying nonchalantly. 'I've done quite a lot. Have you?'

Belinda studied her face critically in the mirror, then added another dab of blusher across her forehead before replying. 'Since I was seven. I don't do much for charity though, they're usually a load of amateurs.'

'Yeah, they are, aren't they?' Donna remarked, as she stroked blusher along her own forehead and down the sides of her jawline the way Belinda had done. Lisa came in carrying a number of dresses over her arm – they all looked incredibly exciting, each one in a polythene wrapper, like Christmas presents waiting to be opened. The girls at the Grove had asked Donna if she'd tried her dress on yet, but Donna had told them airily, 'No need, Lisa says I'm a perfect size ten.' The older girls were of course wearing several different outfits, but as the only young teen model Donna had just the one. 'Don't worry, pet,' her dad had said. 'You'll make much more impact that way.'

'Here we are,' said Lisa cheerfully. 'All newly pressed.'

Holding her breath, Donna carefully removed her dress from its plastic cocoon. Her smile of anticipation froze as she gazed in shocked disbelief at the monstrosity she had revealed. No words could possibly do justice to its sheer revolting naffness. In a babyish pattern of pink and white, it fell in tiers of lace-edged frills to below the knee. There was a matching lace collar, trimmed with horrid little pearl buttons, a wide pink sash fastening in a truly disgusting bow and, worst of all, it had a sticky-out net petticoat that made it look like it was meant to be worn by a particularly yucky fairy on top of a Christmas tree. Nothing, she thought, nothing in the whole world, could possibly be worse than this.

But she was wrong. It could get worse – and it did. In the church hall the packed audience applauded as each outfit in turn made its appearance. Prominent in the front row was a beaming Jim Bell. Lisa floated onto the catwalk wearing a slinky little strapless number, glittering with sequins. She looked good and she knew it. She twirled and blew Jim a kiss before gliding off – straight into a scowling Donna waiting in the wings.

'Right, your turn, pet,' said Lisa.

'I'm not doing it! I'm not! I look a right wally!' Donna wailed.

She certainly looked nothing like the super-trendy Donna Bell who queened it at Byker Grove. Indeed, she looked nothing like the Donna Bell anyone had ever seen anywhere. As if wearing The Horror wasn't bad enough, the organisers had added knee-length white socks, pink ballet slippers and, worst of all, a hideous pink bow in her hair.

The audience was waiting expectantly as the compère announced, 'And now for our Miss Teen model . . .'

'You look very pretty, pet,' said Lisa encouragingly.

'Yuck! I don't want to look blimmin' "pretty", do I?' Donna glared.

But Lisa told her she'd make her dad very proud, and besides, the audience was waiting for her. 'You don't let your audience down, that's the first rule to learn if you're going to be a star,' she added mischievously. Donna had unwisely confided her ambition to Lisa in a weak moment. Now Lisa gave her a firm little shove, and Donna stumbled gracelessly onto the stage in full view of a sea of expectant faces.

Mr Bell nudged his neighbour. 'That's my little 'un.

Looks a proper treat, doesn't she?' he said, bursting with fatherly pride.

Donna stamped furiously along the red-carpeted catwalk with the ridiculous bow wobbling on top of her head. Her eyes were fixed firmly on the floor, which she fervently wished would open up and swallow her.

Then a horribly familiar noise that sounded like a cross between a giggle and a snort made her look up. 'Piggin' heck,' Donna muttered to herself, as she saw Nicola grinning at her fit to burst. Only two more steps, then she could turn round and race back down the catwalk to the safety of the dressing room, where she could tear The Horror off and try to forget the whole sordid episode. The pop of a flash gun stopped her in her tracks. Brad, Cas, Winston, Speedy and Spuggie were bunched together near the stage, and they'd actually had the blimmin' nerve to take her photo! For two pins she'd grab the rotten camera and smash it to smithereens! Giving them a glare that would have splintered glass, Donna turned and ran as fast as her legs would carry her up the catwalk. The bow fell off but she didn't stop to pick it up. All she wanted was to reach the safety of the wings, and hide her scarlet face.

Back at Byker Grove, Rajeev was telling Geoff and Alison about his visit to the Campbell household. As he'd suspected, Geoff wasn't best pleased. 'Why on earth didn't you tell me you were going?' he demanded.

'I thought you might stop me,' Rajeev answered honestly.

'Too true, I would have, you had no right,' Geoff told him. Then he said he'd give the social services a call. Strictly speaking the Grove wasn't supposed to get involved in the kids' home problems, but that didn't stop them giving an unofficial tip-off in the right quarter if anybody was thought to be at risk. 'But you don't go poking your nose into anybody's family life without being asked,' he told Rajeev, adding that before doing anything like that in future he should check with him first.

Alison sprang to Rajeev's defence. 'Maybe he shouldn't have done it,' she said, 'but at least he cared enough to go.' Then she added thoughtfully, 'No wonder those poor kids hang around here every night, always the last to go home.'

It wasn't until later that Geoff heard the full story. 'The lad told me you blew up at him,' Mary O'Malley said, as she put a cup of tea on the desk in front of him. Geoff frowned. 'Rajeev? He had no right to discuss it with you.'

That was when Mary told him he was wrong to blame the boy. She said she was the one who had told Rajeev to go and see Spuggie and Fraser's parents. 'I know you'll say I shouldn't have done it, but what was I supposed to do? Stand by and watch those two poor miserable mites and say nothing? There's far too much of that going on in the world, and far too few as does something about it.'

Geoff was just about to tell her that, much as he sympathised with her point of view, it wasn't always wise for well-meaning outsiders to interfere, when Fraser came running in. For once his face was alight with excitement. 'Me and Spuggie can go to camp now, Geoff,' he said, putting some five-pound notes on the desk. Geoff was delighted that the Campbell kids could join the outing, but as Fraser ran out to find Spuggie and tell her the good news, he turned to Mary O'Malley. 'Where on earth did he get the cash?' he wondered aloud.

Mary had her own suspicions. She caught up with Fraser as he went looking for Spuggie. 'I hope they gave you a fair price for it, lad,' she said shrewdly. She'd guessed correctly that Fraser had sold his precious watch to pay for the trip. At first Fraser tried to pretend he didn't know what she was talking about, but you couldn't hide anything from Mrs O'Malley's sharp eyes.

'Don't tell Spuggie, please,' he begged.

Mary smiled at him, as she said, 'Our secret. So long as you send me a postcard when you get to camp.'

In the general room, Spuggie stared at her brother in disbelief. 'You're not winding me up, Frase? You really mean it?' When she saw he was serious, she flung her arms round him and gave him a great big hug – much to his embarrassment. Then she frowned. 'Fraser? Where did the money come from?'

'Don't ask so many flippin' questions all the time. We're going, isn't that enough?' he muttered crossly, hoping she wouldn't persist. He didn't like lying to her. But he needn't have worried. Spuggie was too happy to pursue the matter.

'Hey, everyone, we're going on the camping trip!' she yelled, dancing round the Grove with her news. THEY WERE GOING TO CAMP! She hugged herself with the blissful anticipation of it all. Spuggie had never had a holiday. They'd gone on a day trip to Whitley Bay once with the Grove, but that was the nearest they'd ever been to a proper holiday. She and Fraser had long since learnt that there was no point in moaning about the way things were. It never got you anywhere. All it did was get dad in a temper if he found out, and nothing was worth that.

It was early evening when Donna finally walked into the

general room, her head held high. She'd been tempted to go straight home, but she knew she had to face them some time, so she might as well get it over. Let them do their worst, she didn't care. A dignified silence, that was the thing. 'One word from any of you and I'll smash you!' The words were out of her mouth before she could stop them, as she saw the grinning faces turn towards her.

'Don't think you've forced Jerry Hall to give in her notice yet,' smirked Nicola.

Alison came out of the office and innocently made things worse as she asked, 'How's our budding fashion model, then? Were you the star of the show?'

'I don't ever want to hear another word about it . . .' Donna began, when she noticed the boys gathered at the far end of the room, apparently playing darts. Only it wasn't a dartboard they were using, but a large photograph. That afternoon, the boys had taken several pictures under Brad's tuition. Most of them were action shots from Walker Wheels, but they'd also taken some at the fashion show, which Brad had already developed in his darkroom. Now Donna remembered the sudden pop of a flash gun as she stared across the room at a hideously large blow-up of herself in That Dress!

Before she could do anything Julie and Gill walked in, hand-in-hand, smiling all over their faces.

'Where've you two lovebirds been?' Cas asked. 'Everywhere, it was brilliant!' a radiant Julie responded, and then stared in astonishment at the blow-up. 'Is that what she wore?' she laughed incredulously. Cas obviously hadn't seen Donna come in, as he grinned back at Julie. 'You should have seen it for real,' he said. 'Especially the cute little bow in her hair!'

That was the final straw. Donna hurtled across the room like an avenging fury and ripped the offending photo off the wall. 'You nerd!' she stormed at Cas. 'Laughing with her about me, behind my back. You've sucked up to her every chance you've had!'

Cas tried to tell her it was only a joke, but Donna wouldn't have any of it. 'I'll give it to you straight, sunshine. If you think you're ever going anywhere near me again, you can forget it!' Her green eyes blazed witheringly at Cas, then she turned and stormed out of the room, leaving the rest of them staring after her in open-mouthed astonishment.

CHAPTER FIVE

It was a fine, bright afternoon, sparkling with spring sunshine. A small knot of people stood on the pavement outside Byker Grove, among them Mr Bell, Lisa and Donna. Jim Bell took a couple of crisp fivers from his wallet and held them out to his daughter. 'There you go, sweetheart.'

Donna wasn't grateful, she was embarrassed. She always had far more money than any of the other kids, most of whom were permanently broke. Flashing her cash around didn't do a lot for her popularity, and being popular was important to Donna. 'I don't need it, Dad. Really. I've got enough.'

Lisa meant well, but Donna really had it in for her now. She'd seen her kissing and cuddling her dad and they seemed to be getting altogether too close. So when Lisa said, 'Take it, pet, we don't want you going hungry,' Donna couldn't help answering nastily, 'Oh, don't we? What's it to do with you? You're not my flippin' mum.' Poor old Jim was caught right in the middle. He'd never willingly make Donna unhappy, but he'd been divorced for some time now, and he needed a life of his own. He was relieved when Donna's friend Nicola rolled up, lugging a holdall.

Nicola looked round and asked casually, 'Is Ian not here yet?' but Donna wasn't deceived. She knew her best friend was getting a bit of a thing for Ian Webster. She also knew she was being horrible by wishing he wouldn't turn up. It would have been different if she and Cas were still going together, but she'd finished with him totally, since she'd caught him laughing at her fashion show photos with Julie Warner of all people. And she didn't want to spend the entire weekend mooching about on her own.

Meanwhile Geoff and Alison had nearly finished loading all the essential supplies into the minibus. Geoff had been to the cash-and-carry and bought cartons of tea, coffee, sugar, breakfast cereal, tinned soups, bacon – all kinds of goodies that could be easily cooked or heated up on primus stoves.

Duncan stood nearby red-faced, wishing his mum wouldn't hang around. She was OK, his mum, but she did *fuss*. She'd even gone through the gear he'd packed, making sure he'd put in an extra sweater and his warm pyjamas. It was *May*, for pete's sake, he'd look a right prat in blimmin' flannelette pyjies. He'd told her he'd be fine in his sleeping bag, but she'd gone on about him having had bronchitis at Christmas – it wasn't bronchitis, it was a flippin' *cough*! In the end he'd had to let her put the horrible things in his holdall, but he wasn't going to wear them, no way. T-shirt and underpants would do great. 'It's all right, Mum, you needn't wait,' he said hopefully, but he knew she'd stick around till the blimmin' bus was out of sight.

Gill and Winston sauntered into view. Bet their mothers didn't make them pack a load of stupid gear they didn't need, Duncan thought.

Donna nudged Nicola. 'Hey-up, trouble's here!'

'I was hoping them two'd miss the bus,' said Nicola loudly.

But Gill was more concerned with looking to see if Julie had by some miracle managed to turn up. She'd put her name down on the list, hoping against hope that she'd be able to persuade her parents to let her go. Winston was hoping against hope she wouldn't. They were going to have a good time, him and his mate. Last thing he needed was that snooty bird shoving her neb in. 'She'll not come, man,' he pronounced, much to

Gill's irritation. 'That mother of hers'll not want her little precious to go camping with rubbish like us.' He got cuffed on the ear for his pains.

A few yards away, an impatient Fraser and Spuggie were sitting on the wall kicking their heels in the sunshine. The Campbells had been the first to arrive, they couldn't wait for the trip to start. Fraser held his breath as Mrs O'Malley trotted down the path from the Grove carrying a large Tupperware container. She was the only one who knew his secret – that he'd sold his watch so that he and Spuggie could go on the camping trip. He'd told his mum and dad and Spuggie that Geoff had arranged for the council to pay for them, and luckily they'd believed him. If his dad had ever known he'd won a watch, he'd have had it off him in a flash. If he'd known he'd won it and *sold* it, he'd have given him a good thrashing.

But Mary O'Malley was as good as her word. 'Don't forget my postcard,' she winked at him, and he knew she was telling him his secret was safe with her.

Nicola breathed a sigh of relief as she saw Ian approaching – for once with no little kids in tow. 'I didn't believe it when you said they weren't coming,' she admitted.

'Me neither,' he grinned at her.

But Nicola's smile faded as her gran came over to them. 'I've made you some buns for the journey, our Nicola,' she said, handing them over. 'There's plenty, so you can share 'em out with your pals.'

Nicola pulled a comical face at the others behind her back, but said, 'Thanks, Gran.' She was feeling too good about things to get into any hassle.

Spuggie wanted to know who she'd be sharing a tent with. Alison said she could go in with Donna and Nicola, and Julie if she showed up.

'We're not sharing with that snobby cow,' said Donna, overhearing.

'Yes you are, Donna.' Alison was sweet but firm.

'Stuck with her and a kid,' Donna groaned. *And* Ian Webster had blimmin' turned up as well. Brilliant trip this was going to be. But there was nothing she could do about it.

Geoff did a head count – they were all there. 'Right, everybody on board.'

'Not all here yet, guv,' said Gill.

Geoff consulted his clipboard again. 'There's only Julie Warner and she knows what time we leave.'

As Nicola headed for the bus Mrs O'Malley warned her sternly not to sleep on damp grass, and to behave herself at all times. 'No funny business, I know what goes on on these trips.'

Nicola giggled and dived into the safety of the bus. What bliss to get away from Gran's nagging for a whole weekend.

Duncan's mum looked at him fondly, and said, 'Have a good time then, lovie. Take care.' Then, to his intense humiliation, she actually attempted to kiss him. His face turned scarlet, aware of a grinning Spuggie watching from inside the bus. 'Aw, Mum, leave it out!' he yelled, and hastily jumped aboard.

Gill was the only one left standing on the pavement. Winston had saved him a seat and was beckoning him to hurry up and Geoff was looking at his watch impatiently. Then at the last minute Mr Warner's car drew up, and Julie leapt out. Grabbing her holdall from the back, she hugged her dad gratefully. 'Bye, Dad. And thanks.' He smiled and told her to enjoy herself.

'I will,' she promised, and climbed onto the bus. Gill grinned as he helped her into the seat next to him.

'Never thought you'd make it, Yorkie. See what happens when you stand up for yourself?'

She sighed, and told him that things still weren't good at home, but he frowned at her and said, 'Listen, Yorkie. You're here now. So forget them and just have a ball, right? And them's orders.'

He looked so stern that she had to hide a smile, and told him she'd try. In spite of everything, she was already beginning to relax, and look forward to the weekend.

Geoff switched on the engine and Winston scowled across the aisle at Julie and Gill sitting with their heads bent close together. Gill was *his* mate – *he* should have been sitting next to him. Drat her. He'd been looking forward to this trip. Why did she have to blimmin' turn up and ruin everything?

As the bus drove off, Mrs O'Malley, Duncan's mum, Jim Bell and Lisa all waved goodbye. Donna scowled briefly, seeing her dad put an affectionate arm round Lisa as they walked away. But she wasn't going to waste any more time worrying about them. She had a plan – she was going to deal with the Lisa Problem in her own way. Meanwhile she had more important things to worry about, like making that rat Cas suffer for all the aggro he'd given her. She pulled a disdainful face as he offered her a toffee.

'No thanks. Save them for your girlfriend.'

'Julie Warner's not my girlfriend,' Cas said patiently. He'd tried more than once to explain that he'd only been joking about the fashion show, he certainly hadn't been laughing at her behind her back, as she seemed to think. He'd also tried telling her there was nothing between him and Julie – she was Gill's bird. But Donna wouldn't listen. Pig-headed women. He sometimes wondered why he bothered with them at all.

Behind the wheel, Geoff started to sing in a loud but tuneful baritone, to the tune from *Snow White and the Seven Dwarfs.*

'Heigh ho, heigh ho,
It's off to camp we go
Just keep on singing all day long
Heigh ho, heigh ho, heigh ho, heigh ho.'

Alison and all the kids gradually joined in, as they left the town behind and headed into the glorious open countryside.

'Heigh ho, heigh ho,
It's off to camp we go
Just keep on singing all day long
Heigh ho, heigh ho, heigh ho, heigh ho.'

Eventually the minibus drove down a particularly winding country lane, and pulled up at the campsite. They were there!

It was a perfect spot, on the site of a ruined priory that dated back to the twelfth century. Thick grey stone walls and archways hinted at how impressive the ancient building must have looked – all those hundreds of years ago. A little way off, the river sparkled in the sunshine. And on the other side of a small wooden bridge, leafy paths wound enticingly into the forest. This was a place for adventure, all right.

The camp was to be pitched on a large grassy clearing, and everybody was rushing around trying to be the first to get their tent up when a familiar little red sports car drove into the campsite.

They hadn't expected Brad, but everybody was delighted to see him. 'Thought you might need an extra hand,' he called over to Geoff. He explained that he had a room at the village pub, as he helped them put up their tents.

A little later, Spuggie and Fraser stood side by side on the wooden bridge, looking at the river as it frothed and glittered in the afternoon sun. For once, they were both perfectly content.

'Isn't this ace, Frase?' Spuggie sighed blissfully. She couldn't wait to splash about, she knew Geoff had planned all sorts of watersports for the weekend. Then she had a thought. 'Hey, you'll be able to try out your watch to see if it really *is* waterproof!'

'I didn't bring it,' said Fraser, looking suddenly uncomfortable. 'Might get broke.'

'That's stupid!' Spuggie retorted. 'It's meant to be shockproof and waterproof, be just the job for here.' But Fraser said that if he didn't want to bring it that was his business, and stomped off back to the campsite. Spuggie shrugged – she was too happy to let Fraser's moods bother her – and ran off to join Duncan on a tyre swing slung from a tree.

While Spuggie and Duncan larked about by the river, Gill, Julie, Ian, Nicola and Winston had walked down to the village to buy ice-cream. As Ian took a photo of the others happily licking their ices, Winston moodily wandered off. He didn't know why he'd bothered to come. Gill had no time for him now, he was too busy making sheep's eyes at Julie Warner.

Suddenly, Winston noticed a girl trying to prop her bike against the wall outside the village shop. More for something to do than anything else, he helped her. She thanked him, and when she went inside, he found himself following her. She was a quiet little thing, not like the girls he usually fancied. But she had big brown eyes and a shy smile, and a way of looking at him that made him feel good. She told him her name was Kelly, and she lived in a farm cottage about a mile down the lane.

She also told him she was fourteen. And when she

101

asked Winston how old he was, somehow he heard himself saying fifteen, although he conceded he was small for his age. After that, things just sort of ran away with him. He couldn't really remember how it began. Perhaps it was when she wistfully said that she wished she lived an exciting life in a big city like him. And he found himself telling her about all the fantastic things he did, the clubs and discos he went to, and his rich dad and all their posh cars and the big house they lived in, with a swimming pool like the Ewings had in *Dallas*. And the more he told her about this amazing life he led, the more her big brown eyes sparkled, and he just couldn't stop . . .

After supper, Geoff led them on a nature trail walk in the woods. It was a beautiful evening, and still light. Ian and Nicola lagged behind, while Ian took her photograph posed against a tree trunk. Then, as Geoff and the kids disappeared round a bend, Ian grabbed her hand and led her in the opposite direction, away from the others.

It wasn't long before sharp-eyed Spuggie noticed their absence. 'Hey, where's Nicola and Ian gone?' she asked in her penetrating little voice.

Before any of them could reply, the penny had dropped. 'Necking, aren't they!' she announced triumphantly. 'They've gone off necking!'

It was Cas who said in an amused undertone, indicating Geoff up ahead, 'Use your loaf, Spuggie.' And he gave a conspiratorial wink at Donna over Spuggie's head. Donna still wasn't speaking to him, but it was all she could do not to smile back.

Meanwhile Ian had led a giggling Nicola into the shadowy privacy of the ruined priory. Shivering in mock fright, she said, 'It's creepy.' But he told her there

102

was nothing to be scared of, and she felt a delicious warmth creep through her as he put his arm round her, and she snuggled up to him. He felt so solid and safe. And yet somehow exciting.

Later, back at camp, it was just getting dark. The kids were sitting round the campfire with mugs of cocoa in their hands. All around them was an unfamiliar silence, broken only by the distant barking of a farm dog. There was none of the traffic noise, the wail of police sirens, the revving up of motorbikes, the raucous singing of drunks, none of the usual night sounds that were a part of the world they'd left behind. Even the familiar background beat of pop music that was a routine part of their everyday lives was missing. Trannies were banned up here. There was just the music they made themselves, as Brad led them all in a rousing chorus of 'Yellow Submarine'.

> 'We all live in a yellow submarine,
> A yellow submarine,
> A yellow submarine,
> And our friends are all aboard . . .'

It had been a lovely day, Donna had to admit. And it was a smashing evening. But she found herself feeling unexpectedly sad as she looked across to where Gill had his arm casually round Julie's shoulders, and Ian was holding hands with Nicola. She thought about her dad and Lisa, and suddenly it seemed as if the whole world was in couples except her. She wished she was at home in her frilly pink bedroom, where she could cry in peace.

Then she sat bolt upright as two hands covered her eyes from behind, and a laughing voice said out of the darkness, 'Guess who?'

It was Cas. But even as she was telling him off for

frightening her out of her wits, she was glad. When he asked, 'OK if I sit here?' indicating the patch of grass next to her, she shrugged and said it was a free country. But she was smiling inside again. It *was* a smashing evening. And she was glad she'd come.

Later, in their tent, Gill, Ian, Cas and Winston were getting ready for bed.

'You seem to be doing all right with Nicola Dobson,' Gill observed to Ian, as he pulled off his trainers.

Ian laughingly hurled his rolled-up jeans at Gill. 'You can talk, you're not doing so bad with that yuppie chick.'

Gill was casual, very laid back. Usually he was the first to boast about his conquests, but somehow this time it was private. 'Julie's OK,' he grunted, then changed the subject by saying to Cas, 'I see you've made it up with Bell's Brewery, then?'

Lying in his sleeping bag, Winston was getting really cheesed off with this conversation. Anybody'd think he wasn't blimmin' *there*. 'I met this bird today,' he volunteered.

They were either too sleepy to reply, or just not interested. He tried again. 'Gave her a right load of codswallop,' he said, very macho. 'You should have heard me. Only told her I was fifteen, and we live in a big house and me dad's got loadsamoney, didn't I?' he added proudly.

Ian was sceptical. 'And she fell for it?'

'Course. She thinks I'm the best thing since sliced bread.'

'So what happens when she finds out you've fed her a right load of old bull?' asked Cas, who couldn't imagine ever having to tell a girl all those fairy stories to get her interested.

But Winston was supremely confident. 'She won't, will she? She lives local, I'll never see her again when we go back. I can tell her anything I want – can tell her Paul Gascoine's me cousin if I want.'

Gill remarked that whoever she was, she must be as thick as two short planks, but Winston denied this. 'She's *not*,' he said huffily. 'As a matter of fact, she's very nice.'

But even as he said the words, it was beginning to dawn on him that he really meant it. And just before he fell asleep, he felt a nasty little premonition hovering in the darkness like an ugly black spider waiting to pounce.

In their tent, Julie and Spuggie were fast asleep, but Donna and Nicola lay whispering together in the semi-darkness, side by side in their sleeping bags. By the shafts of moonlight coming in round the edges of the tent flap, Nicola could see that Donna was wide awake. Her pretty eyes looked troubled as they stared into the night. 'What's up, pet?' she asked, raising herself on one arm. 'Is it Cas? I thought you'd made it up with him?'

'I have.'

'Well then?'

'I was just thinking about me dad. And her.'

'Lisa?'

Donna nodded, and told Nicola that she'd not been too bothered about her dad's other girlfriends because they'd come and gone. But it looked like he was getting serious with this one.

'So?'

'I hate her.'

Nicola was surprised. She knew that Donna was always a bit jealous of any girl her dad paid attention to, but hating was a bit strong. She said as much.

'I don't want him to marry her,' Donna replied sulkily. 'She's not me mum, is she?'

Nicola was nothing if not practical. She explained to Donna that divorced men didn't stay on their own for ever. Her father was bound to remarry some day. And Lisa wasn't so bad. As stepmothers went, she could do a lot worse. Nicola was only trying to help, but Donna angrily told her to shut up. She shrugged – she was used to Donna's mood swings. Then she closed her eyes and promptly went to sleep. But Donna just lay staring into the darkness for a long time.

It was a soft, balmy night. Alison and Brad had strolled away from the campsite and down to the river. They were standing on the small wooden bridge, enchanted by the reflection of the starry sky in the still water.

Alison knew it was a dangerous question, but she had to ask it. 'Why did you come, Brad? It's different for us, we work for Byker Grove.'

'Better than spending the weekend slumped in front of the telly with a takeaway,' he smiled down at her in that lazy way he had. 'But of course if I'm not welcome . . .'

'Don't be silly,' she said, a little too warmly, then was suddenly embarrassed. 'You're very welcome, you know that. The kids are getting very fond of you.'

'Just the kids?'

He held her gaze for a long moment, until she looked away, confused.

'I've got a boyfriend, Brad,' she said finally. And told him about Mike, and what a great bloke he was, and how well they understood each other.

Brad took it all in his stride. 'If you like him, then I'm sure he's Mr Wonderful,' he said. And threw her by kissing the tip of her nose before she could stop him. ''Night, Bright Eyes. Sweet dreams. See you in the morning.'

She watched him drive off in his sports car, still feeling the touch of his kiss. She was more confused than ever.

Next morning Geoff taught them all how to use a canoe, and now Cas, Fraser and Speedy were having a race. Spuggie was jumping up and down with pride on the river bank, as Fraser pulled ahead of the other two.

'He's won, Fraser's won!' she yelled, as if they couldn't see for themselves. 'Get off,' he cried, feigning embarrassment as she gave him a smacking great kiss, but he was grinning all over his face.

Geoff watched as Fraser playfully pretended to throw his sister in the water, and remarked to Alison on the amazing change in the lad. But they were still worried about what would happen when they got home. 'We'll just have to hope the father behaves himself now he knows the social services are keeping an eye on him,' Geoff said.

Alison looked round at all the happy faces, at the kids shrieking with laughter as they swam in the river, splashed about on the water in old tyres, swung from ropes dangling from the trees, or chased each other along the wooded paths, and wondered why it couldn't always be like this for them. She wondered why they had to deal with abuse, and neglect, and drugs and violence and loss of innocence and all the perils of a society that made them grow up too soon.

Later that day, Winston was feeling very much a spare

part again. Gill had mizzled off somewhere with the Julie woman, Ian was smooching with Nicola, and Cas was back with Bell's Brewery. Speedy was kicking a football around on the grass, but Winston didn't feel like joining him. Apart from anything else, he never even got a sniff at the ball when he played with Speedy. Moodily, he walked along the country lane in the direction of the village. A choc-ice might make him feel a bit better.

'Hiya.' Kelly waved to him from the garden where she was hanging clothes on the line. She had five younger brothers and sisters, and had to help her mum a lot of the time.

Suddenly things didn't seem quite so bad after all. Stroke of luck, Winston thought, just bumping into her like that. She came with him to the village shop, and he bought her a choc-ice as well. They cost enough, but he didn't mind. She made him feel really special somehow.

'It's nice talking to you,' she said shyly. 'You're not silly like some of the lads round here, they're just stupid babies. But you're different. I s'pose it's with you being older.'

'Not that much older,' Winston said hastily. The ugly black spider of the previous night had suddenly reappeared. It seemed so real he almost expected her to comment. He could feel it dangling over his head like Little Miss Muffet. 'Er, Kelly, there's something I've got to . . .'

But Kelly was too busy recounting all the wonderful things she'd learned about him to pay any attention. 'And leading such an interesting life and going to all those exciting places abroad and . . .'

Winston was getting desperate. What the heck had he done?

'When are you going to be sixteen, Winston?'

He swallowed hard. 'November 9th.' That at least was true. November 9th was his birthday all right. But he was only going to be fourteen. She was already fourteen. She thought he was nearly sixteen and he was blimmin' *younger* than her. Heck, she'd probably crack up laughing if she knew. Probably call him a stupid kid. A stupid *lying* kid.

'If you give me your address I'll send you a birthday card.'

Did she suspect him? Was she taking the mickey? 'What for?' he asked cautiously.

'Because I want to.' Then she added shyly, 'Because I like you.'

From the way she looked at him, smiling timidly under her long eyelashes, Winston knew that she meant it. That she really did like him and that she believed every word he said. So things couldn't be so bad, could they? He grinned happily as they walked along side by side, and even the black spider went away – for the time being.

Abseiling was a great success. They had to wear hard hats and descend the rockface on ropes secured from above. It looked dangerous but it wasn't really, not when you had people like Geoff in charge. And it wasn't like climbing Everest or anything. These weren't even proper cliffs, just a craggy escarpment on the side of the hill. It was enormous fun but it was also thirsty work.

Geoff looked at his watch. 'Right, that's enough of that for one day. You've all done very well. Now who's going to make a weary old man a cup of tea?'

But as all the other kids headed towards the campsite, Donna hung back. 'You go on,' she called to Cas. 'I'll see you in a bit.'

The phone box was about half a mile down the lane. When she got there Donna pulled a scrap of paper from her jeans pocket and punched out the number she'd written down before she left home. She'd found it in the desk where her dad kept all his stuff. Of course he'd have given it to her if she'd asked, but she didn't want him to know about her plan. Somehow she didn't think he'd be pleased. Still, it was for his own good.

'Mum? It's me. Donna.'

There was a stunned silence at the other end. Mrs Bell hadn't heard from her daughter for over a year, though there hadn't been a day when she hadn't longed to hear her voice. But after she'd left the Byker Arms, Donna had cut her out as though she didn't exist.

'You never answered any of my letters,' Mrs Bell said finally, trying not to sound accusing.

'No, I know I didn't. I'm sorry.' Donna took a deep breath. 'Mum, I can't talk long, I'm calling from a phone box, we're at a camp . . .'

'With Byker Grove? You still go there then? Is it nice?' Mrs Bell knew she sounded pathetic but she desperately wanted to keep her daughter talking. It had been so long. If they could talk, perhaps she could finally make Donna understand. After all, she was a year older now. She was nearly grown up. Then she asked anxiously if something was wrong. There had to be a reason why Donna was making the first move after all this time.

'No, nothing's wrong . . . well . . . it's Dad. He's going with this girl . . . yes, I know you're divorced now, but . . . oh, Mum, I need to see you. I need to talk.'

Donna didn't want to go to Keswick where her mum lived now. She didn't want to meet That Man. So they arranged to meet in The Copper Kettle in Newcastle. It used to be a favourite place of theirs. They'd go shopping in the Metro Centre, then they'd go to The Copper Kettle and make pigs of themselves with big gooey meringues and sticky chocolate eclairs with cream bursting out. All the way back to camp, Donna thought about The Copper Kettle, and what she was going to say to her mum. And how different things were going to be afterwards.

In the woods near the campsite, Julie was picking wild flowers as she and Gill strolled together. She felt happy, much happier than she had in ages. Finchale Priory was a super place. And Geoff, Alison and Brad were great. They didn't come on too heavy, always telling you what to do like some grown-ups did. They *respected* you as a person in your own right, even if you were only fourteen. The kids were OK too, once you got to know them. Even Donna. Not that she and Donna would ever be friends, that would be asking too much. But when she forgot to swank, or be bitchy, she could actually be quite a good laugh. Julie wished she could come out with some of the witty things Donna often said.

'I'm going to press these when I get back,' she told Gill. 'You shouldn't pick them really, but so long as you're careful to leave the roots it's all right, I'll only take a few as a souvenir. . .'

But Gill wasn't listening. He took her by the arm, and swung her round to face him. Then gently, as though she was a piece of fragile porcelain, with one finger he touched her cheek, her eyelashes. He'd known his share of girls, but never one like Julie.

She stood stock still. She could feel the powerful attraction flowing between them, like an electric current. He leaned towards her, and lightly kissed her lips.

111

The kiss became more passionate, and Julie felt herself respond. Then she pulled away. 'Don't, Gill. Please.'

'I thought you liked me.'

'I do like you, Gill. I like you a lot. But we'd better go back.'

For a moment he was angry, but then he smiled. 'You really crack me up, girl, do you know that?'

In silence, they walked back along the path. She couldn't tell him that she was scared. Not of anything he might do, but of the strength of her own feelings.

When they got back to the campsite it was time for the evening meal. Afterwards, while they all helped with the washing up, Spuggie and Duncan described how they had been larking about in a hayrick on the farm, and got chatting to the farmer.

'He said the ruins are haunted,' announced Spuggie importantly.

'Yeah,' added Duncan with relish. 'Old ghost with no head, dressed all monkish.'

'All what?' asked Speedy, baffled.

'He means like a monk,' Cas grinned at Donna. 'Well, he wouldn't be dressed like a flippin' traffic warden, would he? Not in a priory. If it was a *car park* he was haunting . . .'

They all argued over whether or not they believed in ghosts, and Fraser naturally dismissed the whole idea as a scientific impossibility.

'Oh yeah?' said Winston. 'So would you kip the night there, then?'

Fraser only hesitated for a moment. 'Yeah. Why not?'

Winston promptly bet him a quid that he wouldn't. Fraser said he would if somebody else would too. For a few moments it looked as if there'd be no takers, until Gill volunteered Speedy. 'Speedy'll do it. You're not scared of nothing, are you, man?'

112

'No, course not,' said Speedy finally. He dimly suspected he'd been manoeuvred into this, but wasn't quite sure how. And it was too late to back out now. Besides, he *wasn't* scared. Fraser had said there was no such thing as ghosts, and Fraser Campbell knew all there was to know about everything.

It was agreed that much later, when Geoff and Alison had gone to their tents for the night, Fraser and Speedy would creep out with their sleeping bags and spend the night in the Haunted Priory.

Meanwhile, the ancient ruins were the scene of activity of a rather different sort. Nicola and Ian were lying on the grass in the shelter of one of the shadowy archways, indulging in some fairly heavy petting. At first Nicola enjoyed it, but then Ian tried to go too far.

'Stop that,' she said, removing his questing hand. 'I've told you no, Ian. I don't want to.'

'Ah, come on,' he breathed heavily. 'Come on, Nicky. You're not a baby. Don't be a tease . . .'

'I'm not being . . . please, Ian, let me go,' she gasped, and struggling free she ran back towards the camp.

Geoff had called Lights Out for everyone, but in their tent, Ian, Gill and Cas were playing cards by the light of a torch.

'How're you making out with Yorkie Bar, Gill?' asked Ian idly.

'We get along,' said Gill, casually playing a card.

'That's not what he meant,' Cas grinned.

Gill knew perfectly well what Ian meant. The lads always told each other stuff like that, it was nothing new. But he still didn't want to discuss Julie with them. Julie was different.

'She's not a randy little piece like Donna Bell, if that's what you're getting at,' he said to Cas.

For once Cas looked annoyed. 'There's nothing wrong with Donna.'

'Julie's got class,' Gill added, getting further up the other two boys' noses.

'I bet she's frigid.' Ian couldn't resist a macho boast. 'Not like Nicola.'

'Yeah? So how far d'you get with Dobson then?'

'Far as I want to.'

Gill was sceptical. 'I bet.'

Ian was now well and truly needled. 'I'm not all talk like you, Gillespie, just picking little flowers in the wood, I saw you . . .'

They might well have come to blows if Geoff hadn't stuck his head through the tent flap and told them to stop talking, they were keeping the others awake.

The boys would have been surprised if they'd known that in their own tent, the girls were talking in whispers along very similar lines.

Julie wasn't used to talking about deeply personal things, she'd never found it easy. But she was so confused by these new and strange feelings that she desperately needed to sort her head out.

'Nicola?'

'Yes?'

'Does Ian, you know, ever want to go a bit too far?'

Nicola admitted he tried it on sometimes.

'What do you do?'

'Just tell him no.'

Donna hooted derisively at the idea of Gillespie taking any notice of that. Julie was annoyed. 'He does, as it so happens.' She hated the way Donna took every opportunity to put Gill down.

It was Nicola who shrewdly asked, 'So what's the problem, if he stops when you want him to?'

This was the hardest part of all. She knew Donna

would send her up given the slightest opportunity. And Spuggie was lying there with her eyes wide open, determined not to miss a thing. But she just *had* to know if other girls felt the way she did. And how they handled it. 'Sometimes,' she said finally, 'I don't want him to stop.'

She needn't have worried. Nicola at least understood. 'When you feel all sort of warm and tingly, and it's all sexy. And scary,' she sighed.

Then they all admitted it. Even Donna. How it was hard to deal with these feelings, when your body seemed to want to go its own way, like it was something quite separate from your head. But how in your head you knew what could happen if you listened to your body and did something stupid.

'No way am I getting pregnant,' Nicola said firmly. 'My mum made a mistake. She got pregnant when she was nineteen. I don't want to be the same.'

This mention of her mum reminded Donna. She'd kept her secret to herself until now, but it was late, and she was tired, and excited, and not a little afraid. She needed to tell someone. 'I spoke to my mum today,' she said.

'I thought you hated her,' muttered Spuggie sleepily.

'Nose out, Spuggie,' Donna answered, but there was no real heat in her voice. Then she told them, 'I'm seeing her when I get back. She's coming to Newcastle specially.' And hugging the thought to her like a warm, cuddly hot-water bottle, she drifted off to sleep.

Meanwhile two shadowy shapes crept furtively into the gloomy ruins.

'It's a bit, like, dark,' whispered one.

'Course it's dark, it's nearly flippin' midnight,' replied the other.

They started to unroll their sleeping bags.

'You sure you want to do this, Frase?' asked Speedy, not a little nervous by now. People he wasn't scared of – he'd square up to anyone any time. But *Things* were different. You couldn't give a Thing a punch in the gob. Your hand would probably go right through it . . . He went goosepimply at the thought.

But Fraser wasn't worried. 'I'm not giving in to those two clowns,' he said firmly, putting his sleeping bag down on a smooth patch of ground near a high open archway that overlooked the grassy hillside, now obscured as clouds slid across the face of the moon. Speedy sighed, and snuggled down in his own sleeping bag, as close to Fraser as he could get.

A little later, Speedy stirred uneasily. All around them were the secret sounds of the night. Funny, he'd expected it to be dead quiet in the country, but it wasn't. Each night as they'd drifted off to sleep in their tents they'd heard noises, owls hooting, dogs barking, strange chirping sounds of insects. And very early in the morning the cocks crowing. But this new sound he heard was different to any of them.

'What was that?'

'What?' asked Fraser sleepily.

'That.'

They listened. Then they both heard it – a faint rustling, scraping sound.

'Probably a rat,' said Fraser finally. But he didn't sound very convincing. 'A water rat, come out of the river.'

They lay still for a few more moments, every nerve straining to hear. Suddenly the hair on their scalps prickled, as the rustling and scraping were accompanied by an eerie moaning noise.

'Fraser? Rats don't moan . . .'

Fraser was sitting bolt upright, staring at a tall and

ghostly apparition which was silhouetted in the patchy moonlight outside the stone archway.

'Piggin' hell, it's the headless monk!' Speedy couldn't move a muscle, he was petrified. But Fraser was out of his sleeping bag and had sprung to his feet in a flash. He hurled himself through the archway at the 'apparition', bringing it crashing to the ground in a torrent of frightened yells.

'It's not a headless monk,' said Fraser scathingly. 'It's a brainless wally.' Then, as he whipped the sheet off to reveal both Winston *and* Duncan, lying sprawled on the ground, he added, '*Two* brainless wallies.'

'He made me do it, Fraser,' cried Duncan. 'He said I had to let him stand on my shoulders else he wouldn't be frightening enough, I never wanted to, he made me . . .'

Fraser glared implacably down at Winston as he planted one foot on his stomach.

'Two quid,' demanded Fraser, holding out his hand.

'We said one.' Winston managed to look aggrieved in spite of his undignified position.

'Two. One for me, one for him.' Speedy deserved to get something out of this as well.

'All right. Take your flippin' foot off.' Defeated, Winston stood up, rubbing his bruises. Reluctantly, he took two pound coins from his moneybelt and gave them one each, before stomping off back to his tent.

Fraser grinned in triumph, and winked across at a very relieved Speedy, who winked happily back. Ghosts – stupid things – as if anybody believed in them anyway.

All too soon, it was Sunday afternoon and time to pack up.

Geoff was loading up the minibus. 'We want

everything cleared away, no mess for those who come next, please. Always . . .'

'Take your rubbish home,' they all chorused. It had become something of a catchphrase over the course of the weekend, as Geoff had repeated it endlessly.

They were making sure that nothing had been left behind when Nicola came hurtling across the grass like a Polaris missile. Normally Nicola enjoyed juicy items of gossip, but she didn't enjoy the one she'd just heard on the camp grapevine. Not one little bit.

'Hey you!' She stood glaring accusingly at Ian. 'How dare you go round telling everybody I'm a slag?'

Ian had the grace to look ashamed, although he tried to deny it. 'I never!' Maybe he had exaggerated a bit, but everybody did that at camp, didn't they? He tried to explain, but he might as well have saved his breath.

'You're a lying toad, Ian Webster. You think you're a man but you're not. You're just a silly little boy like the rest of them, bragging and showing off the whole time. Well, you needn't brag about me, 'cos you didn't get nowhere and p'raps next time you'll think twice before you open your big fat stupid gob!' And with that she stormed off to sit as far away from him on the minibus as she possibly could.

Unaware of the drama going on a few yards away, Alison and Brad were having a quiet word beside his car. He asked her to ride back to town with him, suggesting tea on the way. She was tempted, but she told him she couldn't. Mike, her boyfriend, was meeting her off the bus.

'Another time, then,' he said, vaulting smoothly into the driving seat and blowing a cheeky kiss as he roared off down the lane.

Most of the kids were now aboard the minibus. Gill was just about to leap up the steps when he nudged

Winston. 'Hey, Win. Isn't that the bird you met in the village?'

Winston looked up to see Kelly coming towards them on her bike. 'I came to say goodbye,' she said, and then added excitedly, 'And I've got something fantastic to tell you!'

'Yeah? What?' asked Winston, with a strange sinking feeling that whatever it was, he wasn't going to like it.

He was right. Kelly told him that her older brother and his girlfriend were going to the Hoppings at the end of June, and they'd promised to take her with them. 'So I can meet you and you can show me Newcastle and all them posh places you go to, and I'll bring my cossie and if it's nice we can go in your swimming pool!'

'T'rific,' said Winston, looking decidedly sick. 'Got to go. T'ra,' he added, as Geoff told them all to get a move on. And, giving her a quick peck on the cheek, he climbed aboard and watched unhappily through the window as she stood there waving until the bus was out of sight.

Across the aisle Julie was unwrapping a small package Gill had given her. Inside was a pretty bracelet.

'It's not much,' muttered Gill, embarrassed for once. 'I got it at that shop in the village.'

But Julie thought it was beautiful. She couldn't have been happier if he'd given her the Crown Jewels. She put it on and promised she'd wear it always.

Further along the bus, Spuggie was telling Fraser what a great time she'd had. Then, looking at him sideways, she added, 'You didn't really leave your watch behind, did you?'

'None of your business,' he said gruffly.

'You sold it so we could come to camp.'

He shrugged. 'It was only a watch.' There was no point in lying any more, now she'd guessed the truth.

'Thank you, Frase. It's been really cool.' She smiled her appreciation, then couldn't help asking anxiously, 'What do you think'll happen when we get back?'

'Nothing. If he starts anything I'll . . .'

But as he tailed off hopelessly, Spuggie had already accepted their lot with resignation. 'We can't do nothing, Frase. We're just kids,' she said sadly.

'Geoff'll help us. Nothing bad'll happen. I promise.'

But behind the manly bravado she instinctively sensed his fear. Spuggie reached out and with a very grown-up, almost motherly gesture took his hand. He allowed her to hold it for a moment, needing the comfort, before pulling away. He'd be fifteen next year. He wasn't a kid. *She* was the kid. She was the one who needed looking after. And there wasn't anybody but him.

Speedy was sitting next to Winston, who hadn't spoken a word since they'd set off, but was just scowling into space.

'What's the problem, Win?' he asked finally. 'If you like her . . .'

'I do.'

'So why don't you want to see her, then?'

Winston's reply was bitter. 'Because I fed her a load of garbage, didn't I? I wanted her to think I was a big man. And now she's coming to Newcastle for the fair and she'll find out I'm only thirteen and me dad's not stinking rich and we don't live in a big house and I've never been on no foreign holidays . . .'

'So don't see her then,' advised Speedy in his usual practical fashion.

'But I *want* to,' said Winston hopelessly.

Speedy was doing his best to understand, but it was hard work. 'So tell her the truth, then.'

'I *can't*,' Winston wailed. 'Oh, heck, what the piggin'

120

hell am I going to *do*, man?'

And he stared unseeingly out of the window, in gloomy despair at the horrible mess he'd got himself into. The big black spider was back with a vengeance, and the worst thing was, there was no one else to blame.

CHAPTER SIX

It was Wednesday afternoon, and Donna and Nicola were just coming out of the Byker Arms on their way to the Grove. Donna looked smugly mysterious, as she said, 'Hey, you'll never guess what me dad's just told me about Hayley!' Donna enjoyed the fact that the Byker Arms was a well-known centre for all the local gossip; she felt that being first in the know added to her status.

Nicola sighed. She didn't enjoy pandering to Donna's airs and graces. 'Go on, then,' she said finally, but Donna hadn't finished yet. 'You've got to swear not to say a word, cross your heart and hope to die!' Nicola privately thought this was being a bit childish, but her curiosity got the better of her, and she impatiently repeated the oath.

'Only he heard this woman saying in the bar, she works the same place Hayley does on her Saturday job . . .'

Nicola had had enough. She told Donna she'd strangle her if she didn't get on with it. 'What did she flippin' *say?*'

Donna looked round. 'Well . . .' she began, and lowered her voice though there was no one within sight . . .

Gill, Speedy, Cas and some of the other lads were kicking a football around on the pitch outside Byker Grove. But Winston sat glumly on the sideline, kept company only by an equally unhappy Popeye, whose lead was tied to the bench. Popeye was just bursting to pull himself free and join in the game.

As she sauntered over to them, Spuggie was feeling pretty down as well, but for a different reason. The

Hoppings started on Friday and she was still as broke as ever. She'd tried everything she could think of, but no way could she make any money. In stupid kids' stories fairy godmothers usually appeared round about now, and made everything OK. Winston didn't look much like a fairy godmother, but she was feeling so desperate that anything was worth a try. 'Have you got any jobs for me, Win?' she pleaded.

He shook his head. 'Sorry. Unles you want to give the allotment another go?'

'Forget that, man.' Disgusted, she walked off, as Winston took a crumpled letter from his pocket and read it yet again. He scanned the words, written in large round handwriting, as if hoping that by some miracle the message might have changed. But it was no use. It still said exactly the same thing.

In the Grove office Geoff was finishing a phone conversation with a mate of his at the social services when Alison walked in. He told Alison they'd been discussing Fraser and Spuggie. 'He's put Les Gardener onto it. If anybody can sort Campbell out he can. Have you seen the size of him? Used to play second row for Gosforth, they called him the Gentle Giant. All bullies are intimidated by anyone bigger than they are.'

'Let's hope so,' Alison said, and added that she'd better tell Rajeev. After all, he had got himself involved on Fraser and Spuggie's behalf – and carpeted by Geoff for his trouble.

'And tell Mary as well, meddling old biddy,' Geoff grinned, then added affectionately, 'Bless her cotton socks!'

In the general room, the 'meddling old biddy' was admiring the bracelet Gill had given Julie at camp. 'Very nice,' said Mrs O'Malley as she handed it back, 'but he's a villain, that lad. You want to watch him.'

'I know Gill's got a reputation, but he's all right with me,' smiled Julie. 'He's taking me to the fair on Friday night.'

Donna was looking forward to Friday too, but for a very different reason. As she came into the general room, she was saying anxiously to Nicola, 'I wonder if she's changed much.'

'Who?' Julie couldn't help asking.

'My mother, not that it's any business of yours.' Donna's mum was coming to meet her in Newcastle on Friday, and she was filled with a mixture of excitement and fear. Supposing her mother had become a stranger? Supposing she just wasn't interested in Donna any more, or in Donna's problems? Supposing she couldn't, or wouldn't help?

In the games room, Winston and Speedy were having a half-hearted game of table tennis. It was half-hearted because Winston missed more balls than he hit. Finally, more to stop Speedy grumbling than because he thought he could help, Winston showed him the letter.

'Who's Kelly?' asked Speedy, puzzled, as he slowly read to the end.

'Girl I met at camp, isn't she?'

'Oh, that's right,' said Speedy, as the light dawned. 'That's good, then, she's coming Friday.'

'No, it's *not* good! I told you on the bus back, don't you remember anything, thicko?'

Speedy struggled with his memory. Then his big, pleasant face lit up. 'Oh, aye. She thinks you're fifteen.'

'And rich,' said Winston, looking glum.

In the letter Kelly had suggested a place and time where they could meet. He could just picture her standing there waiting for him, all excited and happy with that special sparkle in her eyes. What should he do? What *could* he do?

124

'You can't just leave her stood there, Win,' said Speedy, as if reading his mind. 'That's not right.'

Winston tried to think positive. 'Say I do turn up,' he suggested hopefully. 'Say we have an ace time, doesn't mean she has to find out I lied, does it?'

'Course not.' Speedy always liked to make people happy, if he could.

'And say she does find out I lied, that's not so crucial, is it?' Winston was working very hard at convincing himself, but he wasn't having too much success.

When Julie had needed a friend, that miserable time when her mum and dad wouldn't let her come to Byker Grove, Hayley had been there for her. Now Hayley was in trouble – *real* trouble – and it was Julie's turn to lend her support. The only problem was, she hadn't seen anything of Hayley since she'd come back from camp.

Hayley had simply stopped coming to the Grove. When Julie asked if anyone had seen her, Alison said she thought Hayley must be revising hard for her end-of-term exams. Julie knew better. Hayley was probably feeling so miserable she couldn't bear to come to the Grove where the other kids would be laughing and larking around. Julie had tried phoning her at home, but she'd put the phone down when Mrs Oduru had answered – she didn't know how much Hayley had told her mum of the awful predicament she was in, and the last thing Julie wanted was to put her foot in it and make things worse.

But now she could wait no longer. She had to know if her friend was all right. Taking her courage in both hands, she left the Grove and went to the little flat where Hayley and her mum lived. She was relieved when Hayley opened the door.

'Julie!' Hayley was clearly pleased to see her.

'I had to come. You've not been to the Grove for ages,' Julie said nervously. She wasn't sure if Hayley's mum was listening. But it was all right, Mrs Oduru had gone to the library to change some books. Hayley picked up her jacket and the two girls went for a walk along the waterfront, where they always seemed to go when they had a problem to sort out. They both found the river, which wound through the city like a silver ribbon, somehow peaceful and comforting.

'Well? Has anything happened? Have the police . . . ?' Julie stopped. She didn't even like to say the words 'charged you'.

But Hayley said she'd not heard from the hotel or the police since she'd packed her job in. She didn't know if that was a good sign or not.

Julie was shocked when Hayley went on to say she still hadn't told her mum. 'It's been nearly two weeks! She must realise you've not been to work!' she exclaimed.

But Hayley said she'd just gone out in the morning like any normal Saturday, and spent the day mooching round the Metro Centre. 'Then I went home and told her they couldn't pay our wages 'cos the computer had broken down.' She added wretchedly, 'I hate lying to her. I just keep hoping a miracle'll happen and she'll never need to know. Only I know it won't.'

Julie hated to see her friend trapped in such a dreadful situation and feeling so unhappy. She wanted to help, but didn't know how she could, except by keeping Hayley's secret to herself.

But it was already too late. Shortly after Julie said goodbye, telling Hayley she was sure everything would turn out all right, Cas, Gill and Speedy were huddled around Winston in the general room at Byker Grove as he imparted a particularly hot item of gossip. 'I'm telling you, man. Positive fact,' he said, recounting the story with relish.

Cas said he didn't believe it, but Gill wasn't so sure. 'And she always cracks on to be such a goody two-shoes,' he remarked, secretly rather impressed.

Speedy was upset. 'Will they put her in prison?' he wanted to know, as Julie came into the room. Julie pricked her ears up when she heard the word 'prison'. 'What's this?' she asked Speedy. It was Gill who answered. 'They've caught Hayley nicking stuff from that place she works.'

To his astonishment Julie exploded angrily at him. 'She didn't steal anything, you want to watch what you say, spreading dirty lies like that!' she stormed. When she found it had come from Winston, she turned on him, saying he should know better and demanding to know where he'd heard the story.

It was Nicola who accidentally revealed the truth, as she looked at a deeply uncomfortable Donna. 'You made me swear not to say anything!' she exclaimed. But even as Donna was excusing herself, saying it had just sort of slipped out, Julie was yelling furiously at her. 'I might have guessed it was you! Never say a good thing about somebody when you can say something rotten, spiteful cow!'

Donna recovered quickly, as she retorted, 'Don't you talk to me like that, blimmin' Miss High and Mighty.' It might have ended there if Donna hadn't felt it necessary, as usual, to go a bit too far. 'Cracking on to be so much better than the rest of us, we all know what you and Gill got up to in them woods . . .'

That was the last straw. Before anyone could stop her, Julie slapped Donna hard across the face. Donna promptly grabbed a handful of Julie's hair and tugged hard. Within seconds the girls were locked in a no-holds-barred fight, which only stopped when Geoff and Alison rushed into the room alerted by all the screaming and yelling.

Within seconds Geoff had parted the two panting girls. 'I expect this behaviour from some of the lads,' he said, surveying them grimly, 'but I'm surprised at you two. What's it all about?'

Donna and Julie glared at each other, but both remained silent. None of the other kids spoke either. They all felt the Hayley rumour had gone far enough for the moment, they didn't want to cause more trouble by bringing it to Geoff's attention.

Geoff realised he wasn't going to get anywhere. 'Right,' he said, 'if that's the way you want it. But just one thing. Whatever it is, it stops here. Any more fighting and you're both banned from the Grove, is that clear?'

Julie nodded, ashamed of her outburst now, but Donna was still defiant. 'You can't ban me, my dad won't let you . . .' she began, but Geoff frowned. 'I run this place, Donna, not your dad. All right?' And with that he left the room.

Gill grinned at Julie, surprised to see this new side of her. 'By heck, that's a powerful left hook you've got there, Yorkie. I'd not like to get in its way.'

But Julie was still too upset over the incident, and what had led up to it, to be amused. When Brad came in a few moments later with the photos from camp, she could hardly be bothered to look at them, although the others clustered round him eagerly. Donna quickly forgot the fight as she preened over a photo of herself in her swimsuit, though she coyly pretended to be embarrassed. 'Makes me legs look dead fat,' she giggled, though she thought she looked sensational.

'Let me see, let me see,' demanded Spuggie, jumping

up and down. 'Oh, there's Fraser winning the canoe race . . . there's me and Duncan . . .'

Mrs O'Malley looked at Fraser, who was the only one who hadn't joined the group. 'You never told me you won the canoe race,' she said.

'It was a fluke.'

'Eh, lad,' Mrs O'Malley sighed. 'Beats me why you always make yourself out to be nothing much. You're the smartest kid here.' And then she winked at him. 'Apart from me, of course.'

Gill was still trying to cheer Julie up, as he took her over to the snack bar for a coffee. 'Can't wait for Friday night,' he said. But Julie had lost her enthusiasm. She'd been looking forward to it so much but she wasn't even certain that she wanted to go now. It didn't seem right enjoying herself at a funfair, when Hayley would be having such a miserable time.

Gill tried to convince her. He told her the Hoppings wasn't just any *ordinary* funfair, it was magic, it was like nothing else in the whole world.

'Wish I was going,' Spuggie muttered mournfully, when she heard Gill talking to Julie. Mrs O'Malley was surprised. She knew that all the Byker Grovers, in fact all the kids from miles around, would be there. It wasn't like Spuggie to miss anything, let alone anything as exciting as this.

'I've got no flipping money,' sighed Spuggie. 'It's all right for people like Julie and Donna, they get everything they want. I can't even get a blimmin' titchy *job*!'

The next morning, Mrs O'Malley was wheeling her shopping trolley past the Byker Arms when she saw Jim Bell glaring in annoyance at some garish graffiti that had been painted on the pub walls the previous night. 'They want to bring back the birch for them brainless young louts,' said Mary. 'And national service. And hanging,' she added with satisfaction.

'Don't worry, Mary, if I get my hands on 'em they'll learn a lesson they'll not forget in a hurry,' Jim promised, tutting in annoyance as he complained that he had quite enough to do without having to spend hours scrubbing off graffiti.

Mary had an idea. 'What's it worth if I get the job done for you?'

Jim tried unsuccessfully to hide his amusement. 'I don't think it's quite your scene, Mary.'

'Not me, you daft wassock,' she retorted with spirit. 'But there's somebody I know'd be only too happy to clean it up – for the right price.'

Which was why, later that afternoon, Spuggie and Duncan were to be found up to their elbows in soap suds outside the Byker Arms as Jim Bell came out with lemonade and crisps. 'Mind you make a good job of it, kids,' he smiled.

'We will, Mr Bell,' smirked Duncan. 'Be so clean you could eat your dinner off them walls.'

'Crawler,' scoffed Spuggie, as Jim went back inside. 'Be so clean you could eat your dinner off 'em. Whoever eats their dinner off blimmin' *walls*!'

Duncan grinned as he threw his wet cloth at her. She promptly threw her soggy sponge at him. Challenged, he picked up a bucket of soapy water and held it at a threatening angle. Spuggie wasn't going to be intimidated, no way. She picked up the hosepipe and, turning the spray to full on, advanced towards him with a wicked smile on her face . . .

In the girls' loo at the Grove, Nicola and Donna were giggling together. Donna's head was completely encased in silver foil.

'Right, time to wash it off,' announced Nicola, looking at her watch.

'Best give it another few minutes just to make sure,' Donna replied, as Julie came in. There was an awkward silence for a moment. This was the first time they'd met since the fight. Nicola took charge. 'All right, you two, no bashing each other today else I might have to step in and clobber the both of you,' she grinned. Julie was grateful to her – *she* certainly didn't want to keep up this stupid feud. 'What are you doing?' she asked, anxious to change the subject.

Nicola explained that Donna wanted to look really good for when she met her mum the next day. She couldn't do it at home for fear her dad might see. 'He'd go bonkers,' grimaced Donna. 'He hates me messing with me hair and he's in a foul enough temper as it is with that stuff somebody's painted all over the pub.'

'What colour's it going to be?'

'A sort of cross between Madonna and Kylie Minogue,' Donna answered optimistically.

'With a touch of the Tina Turners thrown in,' grinned Nicola. Julie grinned back, relieved that everything seemed to be back to normal.

She wouldn't have been so happy if she'd known that in the general room the gossip about Hayley had started up again. This time it was Rajeev who was furiously telling Winston that he could get into serious trouble for spreading malicious rumours. Winston was unrepentant – he was only repeating what Donna Bell's dad had heard in the Byker Arms.

'Pub gossip from someone who was probably half cut,' Rajeev interrupted scornfully. They were all so involved in the argument that none of them noticed Hayley walk in.

Cas repeated that he still didn't believe it, and neither

did Fraser. But Gill said, 'Why not? Nobody's a blimmin' saint, and she *is* a nig nog . . .'

Rajeev was dangerously quiet as he told him to shut up – and it was only then that they saw Hayley. The room fell silent as, with her head held high, she walked over to the snack bar and asked Mrs O'Malley for a cup of tea.

In the girls' loo, Nicola was finally about to wash the gungey stuff off Donna's hair when one of the other girls raced in. 'Hayley's just come in and Rajeev and Gill are bashing hell out of each other!' she announced dramatically, if not exactly accurately.

'What?' exclaimed Julie, and rushed out of the room. Nicola couldn't resist seeing what was going on, and followed her.

'Hey, wait for me!' called Donna, hot on their heels, completely forgetting that her head was still encased in silver foil.

In the general room Hayley was outwardly very composed, as she coolly announced to the assembled kids, 'They found the ring. I suppose you all know what I'm on about?'

There were embarrassed murmurs from some quarters.

Hayley went on to tell them that the woman had dropped the ring down the lining of her bag. 'So for all those who thought I was a tealeaf, I'm not, OK?'

The somewhat ashamed silence that followed was broken by Cas, who had just caught sight of Donna. 'Flamin' Norah,' he hooted. 'The Martians have landed!'

The tension was broken as everybody laughed, while Donna, suddenly realising how she looked, went crimson with embarrassment and rushed out of the room. In the doorway she collided with Spuggie, who asked with interest, 'What have you got on your head, Donna?'

'Oh, naff off!' said Donna rudely, hissing at Nicola to come and help her wash the stuff out.

But Spuggie was too happy to be offended, as she waltzed up to Fraser and offered to treat him to a Coke and a Kit-Kat. 'It's all right, I'm buying them,' she said, as he frowned anxiously. 'It's a present for taking me to camp.' And she waved a five-pound note under his astonished nose. 'Mr Bell gave it us for cleaning his walls, so I can go to the Hoppings now,' she told him. And added to Mrs O'Malley, as she handed her the drinks and biscuits, 'Wasn't that ace of him?'

'Ace,' confirmed Mary, deadpan. If Spuggie had but known it, fairy godmothers come in some unlikely guises.

Julie took Hayley to a quiet corner of the room and asked her what had happened. Hayley explained that the manager of the hotel had phoned and told her about the ring being found. 'Thank goodness me mum was out. He didn't exactly apologise, 'cos according to him he'd never actually accused me. But he said I could have my job back if I want it.'

'What did you say?'

Hayley grinned and said she'd been tempted to tell him what he could do with it, but after all it was a job. They needed the money. 'And if I go back my mum need never know anything about it.'

Julie hugged her. She was so glad that everything had turned out all right in the end.

In the girls' loo, Donna was staring at the mirror with dismay.

'It's not so bad,' said Nicola not very convincingly, as she eyed the mass of orangey-red frizz which now crowned Donna's head. She tried unsuccessfully to stifle a giggle. 'Dunno about Madonna, you look more like Rod Stewart.' Donna wasn't amused – she threw her such a vicious look that Nicola hastily added it might help if she washed it again. But Donna had already washed it six times; nothing seemed to make any difference.

'I said you'd left it on too long, didn't I?' Nicola reminded her smugly.

'Oh, shut it, know-all,' Donna replied, then added bitterly, 'I'll just have to wear a blimmin' hat for the next six months.'

'What will your dad say?'

'It's what me mum'll say that worries me.' She groaned as she looked into the mirror again. 'I just wanted to look nice for her tomorrow, that's all . . .'

The first day of the Hoppings dawned bright and sunny. The whole city of Newcastle was buzzing with anticipation. This was the biggest fair in the whole country. The tradition had begun way back in Victorian times, and for the next ten days the fair would spread like a giant colourful patchwork quilt right across the side of the Town Moor.

As Alison walked into the Grove that afternoon, she was surprised to meet Brad in the hall. 'Hi, what are you doing here?' she asked him. 'There's no photography tonight, is there?'

He told her there'd be no point, all the kids would be at the fair later. 'Actually, I came to see if *you're* going along.'

Deliberately misunderstanding him, Alison said she wouldn't be, as her boyfriend Mike was working late. They'd probably go sometime over the weekend. She was scared of her growing feelings for Brad, and felt guilty because she was still very fond of Mike.

'I'm available as stand-in if it wouldn't be treading on his toes,' Brad offered.

Alison was tempted. It wasn't like a proper *date*. All the kids would be there. Everybody. It wasn't as if she was going off somewhere quiet with him on her own.

'Candyfloss? Hot dogs? Toffee apples?' he murmured.

She had to laugh. 'How did you know I was addicted to toffee apples?' She hesitated only a moment more. 'OK, if Geoff can spare me,' she said finally.

Brad pointed out that the Grove was three-quarters empty already. Indeed, as they listened there was none of the usual excited hubbub coming from the general room. In fact the big old house had an unfamiliar deserted air to it, as though for once it had been left in peace to its memories and its ghosts. Tonight, the excitement was to be found somewhere else.

Outside the Grove, the kids were meeting up – they were going to the fair in a gang. Naturally Spuggie and Duncan were the first to arrive, and Spuggie called impatiently to Fraser as he came out of the Grove, 'Let's go, then, it'll be starting!' But Fraser said he wasn't going. Spuggie was concerned. She hadn't forgotten how he'd sold his watch so that the two of them could go to camp. Now it was her turn to be generous. 'If it's 'cos you've got no money I'll buy you a ride,' she offered. 'Big Wheel, Waltzer, you can choose.'

But Fraser's pride wouldn't let him allow his little sister to spend her hard-earned money on treats for him. The cash she'd made from washing the Byker Arms walls would be just about enough to let her have a go on her favourite rides. He wanted her to have the best time she could.

'No, it's OK,' he said. 'I really don't want to go. I've

got a book I want to read.' He saw the doubtful look on her face. 'Not everybody's potty about fairs, you know,' he grinned at her reassuringly. As he walked away, Cas and Speedy arrived together, soon followed by Nicola, who said that Donna was meeting them at the fair later.

'Why, where is she?' Spuggie demanded, nosy as ever.

Nicola explained that today was the day Donna was seeing her mother, and they all set off, with Spuggie and Duncan racing excitedly on ahead. Gill said he'd wait for Julie, he was sure she wouldn't be long.

But the fair was the last thing on Julie's mind as she looked at her parents in shocked disbelief.

'Divorce?' she gasped. She'd known for a long time that things weren't right at home, but nothing had prepared her for anything as dreadful as this.

They took it in turns to explain that they'd had problems long before they'd moved to Newcastle. 'We'd hoped a change of scene would make things better . . .' Julie's mum said.

'So why didn't it?' Julie demanded.

Mr Warner and his wife looked sadly at each other. 'Because we've grown too far apart.'

'Don't you love each other any more?' Julie asked, fighting back tears.

They both said that they did. 'We always will,' Mrs Warner added.

'But not enough to stay together,' Julie exclaimed bitterly.

Then they explained that Julie and her mum would be going back to live in Wimbledon, while Mr Warner would stay in Newcastle. 'I'm going to look for a nice little flat for the two of us, we can go down together and . . .' Mrs Warner began.

'When?'

Her mum told Julie the sooner the better, in fact she'd thought they could drive down that evening and spend the weekend flat-hunting.

'I can't. I'm meeting my friends at the fair,' Julie said in a bleak voice. She wasn't really interested in the fair any more, but right now it seemed important to be with the others. The thought of being with Gill and Hayley and Nicola, even Donna, somehow seemed safe and reassuring in this suddenly terrifying world.

Mrs Warner said that was no problem. She'd pick her up at the Hoppings and they'd drive to London from there.

Lights, noise, music, laughter and great swirling masses of colour – these were the first impressions a visitor had as they approached the Hoppings.

Outside the entrance to the Ghost Train, Winston stood waiting apprehensively, his fingers crossed behind his back.

'Hi! I made it!' Kelly ran up with a smile all over her face. 'Did you get my second letter? Only we couldn't come this afternoon after all 'cos Donald had to work, so I won't be able to see your house and your swimming pool and that.'

'I know. Shame,' said Winston, hoping he sounded sufficiently disappointed.

'At least we can be here together.' She looked round at the vibrant spectacle with shining eyes. 'Oh, Winston, isn't it *fabulous*! What shall we go on first?' And as they raced off to buy tickets for the Ghost Train, Winston began to relax. Perhaps there was nothing to worry about after all.

Meanwhile Spuggie and Duncan were whirling happily about on the Dodgems. As the ride ended they looked up at the Divebombers curving a dizzy arc in the sky. Spuggie yelled, 'Come on, Dunc! Dare you to go on!', while over on the carousel, Alison and Brad sat happily astride the great painted horses as they bobbed up and down to the traditional music of the fairground.

Someone who wasn't sharing in the general happiness was Gill. He stood outside the Grove, moodily kicking stones as he looked at his watch for the umpteenth time. Where the heck *was* she? He hoped her blimmin' mother hadn't put her spoke in again.

At the fair, Cas, Nicola and Speedy were staggering off the Waltzer. 'Oooh, I think I left me stomach behind,' Nicola groaned. Then she asked Cas what the time was.

'Quarter past six,' he replied. They'd arranged to meet Donna at half past.

'What time's she meeting her mum, then?' asked Speedy. Nicola said she was seeing her at five. 'Wish I was meeting my mum,' Speedy said, looking unusually wistful for a moment. But he quickly brightened again as they sped off to see the sideshows and the Tallest Man on Earth.

A mile or so away, Gill gave one final, furious look up and down the road. There was no one in sight – at least, no one with short brown hair and dark eyes who answered to the name of Julie Warner. Needing to vent his anger and disappointment on something, Gill picked up a brick and hurled it at the Grove. He didn't even look back at the sound of breaking glass as he angrily strode off down the street.

It wasn't that Julie had forgotten she was supposed to be meeting Gill. But right now she needed to talk to a girlfriend. Someone who knew what it was like to come from a – what was that horrible phrase they used? – 'broken home'. That was what it was going to be from now on, she might as well get used to it.

Hayley was just about to set off for the fair when Julie knocked on the door. Now, they were walking along together, and Hayley listened sympathetically as Julie recounted what had happened. 'You know what the worst part is? Having to choose between them,' she finished.

Hayley was surprised. 'Did they say that?'

Julie shook her head, and explained that both her parents took it for granted she would go to live with her mother. 'Of course I want to, I can't imagine not being with her. But Dad needs me too. Mum can cope on her own. Dad . . . he's helpless. He'd live off cold baked beans. And as for ironing a *shirt* . . . ,' she added hopelessly. 'I hate to think of him on his own. He's no good on his own.'

Julie suddenly became aware of the jostling, laughing throng around them, as crowds of people streamed towards the fair. Sunk in her own gloom, she'd hardly noticed where she was. She remembered that she was supposed to be meeting Gill and the others. 'But I don't feel like going now,' she sighed.

'Course you do,' Hayley smiled. 'We've both had enough of problems, time we had some fun.'

Julie found herself smiling back. 'You're right. Pigging problems,' she grinned. 'Let's go and have some pigging fun!'

And Hayley had to laugh at the usually ladylike Julie's choice of words, as the pair of them walked off arm in arm towards the Town Moor.

At the coconut shy, Winston was trying to win a fluffy rabbit for Kelly. 'Isn't he cute?' she'd remarked.

'You want him?' Winston was feeling terrific. So far things were going great, he'd been a right wally to have given himself all that hassle for nothing. 'I'll win him for you,' he promised, very laid back.

Kelly's adoring gaze was the only incentive he needed. As he hurled the balls at the coconuts with all his strength, Hayley and Julie walked past on their way to find the other Byker Grovers. Just at that moment, Winston finally won the coveted prize. Seeing the stallholder handing it to him, Hayley couldn't help it. 'Hey, Winston,' she giggled, 'thirteen's a bit old for bunny rabbits.'

Blithely unaware of the bombshell she'd just dropped, Hayley walked on as Winston looked appalled at Kelly.

'Thirteen? But you said . . .'

There was nothing for it. 'I lied,' he admitted wretchedly. He may as well get the lot off his chest, he had nothing to lose now. 'I lied about me dad being rich as well, we don't live in a big house with a swimming pool and I've never been abroad . . .' He glared at her belligerently, but she just stood there staring at him. 'Well? Aren't you going to sling your hook?'

'Why?' she asked in a small, clear voice.

'Aren't you mad at me for giving you all that bull?'

'Why did you?'

'I just wanted you to think I was, like, something a bit special.'

She smiled at him then. 'I do think you're special, Winston. And I'm glad you're not rich. We're not rich, we're dead poor. Me dad's been out of work for yonks. I like it better that we're the same.' She tucked her arm through his. 'And I love my rabbit. I'm going to call him Winston.'

Nicola, Speedy and Cas were buying candyfloss

when they spotted a moody-looking Gill walking round on his own.

'Where's Julie? I thought you were meeting her?' said Nicola.

Gill muttered something about having changed his mind. A man was better off at the fair on his own, he sneered, without girls shrieking they were scared of this and scared of that the whole time. It was much more cool to be on your tod.

Nicola wasn't fooled for a moment. 'You mean she stood you up,' she sniggered.

'Weird, that,' commented Speedy. 'Donna's stood Cas up as well.'

'She's never. She's just a bit late, that's all,' said Cas, trying to hide his anxiety. It wasn't like Donna to miss all the fun.

Far from having fun, Donna had been sitting alone in The Copper Kettle, the dregs of a strawberry milkshake in front of her. She'd managed to tone down her fiery hair colour, but that wasn't uppermost on her mind right now. The waitress asked if she wanted anything else, but she shook her head. She just sat there with her eyes fixed hopefully on the door. She'd been waiting for nearly two hours now, but although lots of people came into the café, none of them was her mum.

Finally she looked at the clock for the last time. It said a quarter to seven. She had to face it, her mother wasn't coming. Throwing some money down on the table, she walked out into the street.

Julie and Hayley found the others by the candyfloss stall, where they were still waiting for Donna.

'Where the hell were you . . . ?' Gill began angrily, but Julie said she'd explain later. He'd planned to give her a good telling-off, but something in her face stopped him. Instead he bought her a giant stick of sugary-pink candyfloss.

Just then Rajeev walked past, on his own. He'd come with some pals but they'd got separated in the huge throng. 'Like looking for a needle in a haystack in this mob,' he grinned. Hayley said they were all going on the Big Wheel, as soon as Donna turned up. 'You might spot them from up there.' She was pleased when Rajeev said that was a great idea. She admired Raj, and Julie had turned out to be a great mate, and she'd got her job back, and everything was looking really good.

A little way away, Brad was waiting for Alison as she came out of the fortune teller's booth. 'What did she say?'

Alison grinned. 'Strictly private.'

They walked along silently for a few moments, just happy being there together. Suddenly Alison turned and on impulse kissed Brad lightly on the cheek.

'What was that for?' he asked, surprised but pleased.

'Cos I felt like it!' she said demurely.

'In that case . . .' he pulled her to him, and kissed her again. This time it was much more passionate and loving. Spuggie and Duncan passed by and giggled, but raced on. There were much more interesting things to do at the fair than watch a couple of grown-ups snogging.

Mrs Warner's car pulled up as Julie came into sight.

'Jump in, love,' her mum said as she opened the passenger door. 'I've packed a flask and some sandwiches. With any luck we'll be there before midnight.'

Julie didn't hesitate. She knew what she had to do. 'I'm not coming, Mum,' she said.

Mrs Warner was surprised. 'Oh, I thought you'd

enjoy helping me find a place for us to live . . .' she began, but Julie interrupted her. She told her mum there would be no point in her going flat-hunting in London because she wouldn't be living there. 'I'm staying here in Newcastle with Dad,' she said.

Her mother struggled to understand. 'But you're growing up. It's not an easy time. A girl needs her mother around.'

Julie saw her own tears mirrored in her mother's eyes as she answered, 'She needs her *parents* around, but if they're not together then she's got to choose, hasn't she?'

She kissed her mother's cheek. 'I do love you, Mummy, but I love Daddy too, and he needs me. I'm staying here with him.' She didn't add 'and with all my new friends', but as she walked back to rejoin them, she realised how much that was a part of it too.

They all gave a small cheer as Donna finally arrived at the candyfloss stall. Nicola took her to one side and asked what had happened.

Donna couldn't hold back any more. It all came pouring out. 'It's horrible. I don't want my dad to marry Lisa. I don't want him to marry anybody. I want my mum to come back. That's why I wanted to see her today, to ask her to come back and be like we used to.'

Nicola was stunned. She'd had no idea of what had been in Donna's mind – Donna had always made such a thing about not caring what happened to her mum. Now she understood just how much her friend had been pretending, and how hard it must have been for her all this time. 'So what did she say?' she asked gently.

There was a long silence. 'She never showed up,' Donna admitted finally.

'Oh, Donna.' Nicola put her arm round Donna's shoulders. 'Oh, Donna, pet, I'm so sorry. I really am.'

But Donna wasn't Donna for nothing – she wasn't going to let the rest of the world see that she was down. With a huge effort she sniffed back the last of her tears, and bravely painted a bright smile on her pretty face. 'Hey, Cas!' she yelled above the raucous din of thousands of happy voices and fairground music. 'Are we meeting the others at the Big Wheel or what?' And both she and Julie forgot their unhappiness as they all raced off to keep the rendezvous they'd arranged beforehand with the rest of the gang from Byker Grove.

Approaching the Big Wheel, they saw Winston, Kelly, Hayley, Rajeev, Duncan and Spuggie waiting for them. Donna and Nicola grinned and hugged each other as Brad and Alison appeared, hand in hand.

The Big Wheel went round and round, and passers-by smiled at the excited faces as they sat two by two in the gaily painted scarlet and gold carriages – Gill with his arm round Julie, Donna clutching onto Cas, Winston and Kelly, Nicola and Speedy, Duncan and Spuggie, Hayley and Rajeev, Alison and Brad. They all shrieked with mingled terror and laughter as the Wheel spun in its dizzying circle, soaring high up, up into the sky and then swooping down, down to the ground in a way that left your stomach right up there in the clouds.